ANTIQUITIES

ANTIQUITIES

A SEQUENCE OF SHORT STORIES BY

Val Mulkerns

ANDRE DEUTSCH

First published 1978 by
André Deutsch Limited
105 Great Russell Street London WC1

Copyright © 1978 by Val Mulkerns

Printed in Great Britain by
Lowe & Brydone Printers Ltd
Thetford Norfolk

ISBN 0 233 96971 3

To the memory of Frank O'Connor

'We present not these as any strange sight or spectacle unknown to your eyes who have beheld the best of Urnes and noblest variety of Ashes; Who are yourself no slender master of Antiquities and can daily command the view of so many Imperiall faces; Which raiseth your thoughts unto old things and consideration of times before you when even living men were Antiquities; when the living might exceed the dead and to depart this world could not be properly said to go unto the greater number.'

Sir Thomas Browne *Urne Burial*

Contents

A Bitch and
a Dog Hanging

THE nearest I ever came to a country childhood was at
Sheeran's place. Practically every girl I knew at school had
at some time or another spent long holidays in the west or
south, with grandparents, uncles or aunts. My relations all
lived within a stone's throw of the city and when one went
to stay with them it was just like at home except that there
were more treats, less food and no discipline at all. It was, in
short, very agreeable, but years later when I first went to the
west of Ireland and learned about people who live according
to the natural rhythm of the seasons I knew I had come
across their lives before, at Sheeran's place.

One Sunday when I'd been married four or five years and
when the restrictions of new motherhood began to irk me
more than usual, I picked a quarrel with Denis (which was
difficult) and drove, not into the mountains for a long walk
as was my usual habit, but across the mutilated city from the
Victorian south suburb where I live. I didn't try to find the
house where I grew up among a desolation of similar small
houses with no trees in sight except the sycamore which my
father gradually allowed to take over the garden. I never
wanted to see that house again, but what I would have loved
to know I could find was Sheeran's place, whitewashed
among its green fields, with a sloping thatched roof that
was cross-patched with straw of varying colours. Behind it
used to be the byre, the piggery, the kitchen garden and the
strange evil-smelling dry lavatory with rose bushes flourish-
ing around it. Sheltering the farmhouse were lines of beeches,

some of them very old, but not so old as the single chestnut tree that stood in the middle of the fields. It was like a cathedral, like a world of its own when you were small and stood staring up into its living green twilight. Magpies lived there and smaller birds of every kind and a colony of rooks. I remembered their circling about the farmhouse in the smoky pink sky before bedtime every evening; I remember their raucous yet friendly voices. In the loft where I slept in an old settle I could hear them before I dropped asleep, drunk with fresh air and the multiple pleasures of a world I hadn't known existed.

Mick Sheeran (always referred to by his wife as 'Sheeran') had made a swing for my brother and me there and I remembered him trying for a long time to loop a thick rope high enough up in the branches. I remembered how patiently he went on trying although he cursed aloud sometimes when it kept falling down and I remember his bellow of triumph when at last he had a swing actually operating for us. He fetched an old brown horse blanket from the house and made a seat softer than the rope for us and then (putting my brother gently aside with the reproof, 'Ladies first, if you please, young sir,') he lifted me onto the cushion and sent me soaring up into the very body of the tree, part of its gloom, part of its mystery, free as the birds that flitted constantly to and fro among its intricate green leaves backlit by the sun. On the up stroke I was higher than the house; I could look over the thatch at the tops of the trees behind, at the blue mountains on the other side of the city. When I swung down again my stomach fell first in a sickening heave and sometimes I shouted to Mick not to push me any higher while at the same time half-hoping he would. Once I looked right into the face of a startled wood pigeon and once the toes of my sandals cracked off a small dead twig left over from the winter gales. The branch on which the swing depended often creaked and shook, but Mick Sheeran said it would never break. Even years ago, when his own children were small, it had held them. It held them still when they were big fellows finished with school.

Below me where I swung happy as a queen my brother
restlessly paced, tugging at Mick's sleeve to know if it was
his turn, shouting in a way he knew was futile at me to come
down. Up there in the green drunken gloom a kind of mad-
ness would take hold of me. Fair play meant nothing to me
any more. I shouted to be given five minutes longer, two
minutes, and then my brother would begin to blubber and
Mick's sense of equity would be touched. He would grab
me as I swung past him and it would be over, the sense of
power and freedom, of belonging where one had no right to
be, not being a bird.

It's hard to believe now that it didn't go on all summer. It
went on for precisely two weeks and when we went sadly
home again to the narrow streets it was to a usurper in the
house. My mother had her second and last son to look after,
an unbelievably small ugly creature called Fergus who cried
most of the day and all night and created a completely
different house for us to live in. Only Mrs Sheeran whom
we called Nanny was the same. She was not, of course, a
children's nurse, merely a large-hearted charlady who came
to us three days a week and happened to have been known
to everybody always as Nanny although her name was Anne.
She was not a farmer's wife either, which is why she went
out to work for another family as well as ourselves. Sheeran
was a herdsman for a landowner called Ffrench whose grandfather had built the Sheeran house for another herdsman.
The Big House which Mick Sheeran sometimes spoke about
was all of two miles away across the fields, and we had never
even seen it. Mr Ffrench paid poor wages, my father said,
but a large family of Sheerans was reared on the pickings.
No fresh meat or vegetables or milk ever had to be bought,
no flour or bacon or potatoes. I often wonder now what sort
of 'arrangement' was made for our keep during those two
weeks when my mother was in the nursing home. Could
such princely entertainment as we were given be bought for
money? Was Nanny paid double or treble wages for those

weeks or was she paid just the usual weekly sum which she earned in a different way – by keeping us children rather than cleaning our house? Who at this stage knows? It is more than likely she refused indignantly to take an extra penny – wasn't she only doing what she'd do for any neighbour in the same circumstances? Maybe my mother gave her a big tin of biscuits when she got back home and maybe my father sent Sheeran a bottle of whiskey. At the time such questions never occurred to me.

Nanny was my contact with the green fields which I'd been told had once rolled up nearly to the edge of Dublin Castle. In the classroom, on the wireless, in a book, I would come across the magic word 'country' and it was Sheeran's place I would see, the black pig that for some unknown reason preferred to eat sweet pea in Nanny's flower garden than nourishing swill in the piggery; the hen which would lay nowhere but in a certain bush near the oak tree where we could find the eggs and carry them carefully back to the kitchen; the red calf we had seen being dropped the very day before we went home. The mystery and excitement of that stupendous event is forever mixed up in my mind with the monotony of my young brother and the sense of shock that both my parents were pleased about him.

That the winter which followed was not much different from the others was entirely because of Nanny Sheeran. Our Saturdays, in particular, were exactly the same. Always on Saturday my parents went out together, usually to a matinee performance at the Abbey Theatre, and then Nanny would feed and change the baby and hush him to sleep by some magic of her own, not to waken again until my mother's voice sounded in the hall. Once his nagging cry had stopped, the old peace and sense of fun descended on the little kitchen again. By this time the housework would be finished apart from the ironing, and the Sheerans' Sunday joint would be sizzling away in our oven. There was a proper gas oven out in the scullery but Nanny preferred the old kitchen range which twice a week she blackleaded to make it shine. She didn't open up the little door on Saturdays (as we always did to watch the glowing coals inside the bars) because that would be diverting heat away from the oven, but it was always warm in the kitchen anyway and dusky even in summer because of the sycamore. Sometimes when Nanny did the ironing the heat was overpowering but we never complained as we might to our mother. Heat and half-darkness and for long periods silence were part of those magic afternoons. Nanny for a lot of the time was probably very tired. She sighed often and pushed back wisps of hair from the small lined face that had weak red-rimmed eyes: in winter her eyes were often watering. But her smile was something to remember. She had no teeth but didn't show the bare gums. Her mouth turned up moistly at the corners and crinkled like the small old eyes. I never before or since saw anybody's hands so seamed and shrunken yet so clean. Had rubber gloves not been invented then? If so, Nanny Sheeran never heard of them. Her hands were constantly in and out of hot water and carbolic soap, washing floors, cleaning out fires, blackening ranges and polishing brasses. On the days of the week when she didn't work for us she worked even harder for the wife of a government minister whose living-in help wouldn't touch rough work of any kind. Nanny complained sometimes and other times laughed about the heap of old newspapers the minister's lady commanded to be left in the corner of the kitchen. They had to be lifted out of the way when the floor was being scrubbed and put back again when the job was finished. Some day, she told Nanny, some day she would sit down and read all her husband's speeches in Dáil Éireann and then the big bundle could be thrown out. 'That'll be the day,' Nanny used to chuckle to my mother. 'That'll be the day, ma'am, when pigs will take wing and fly.'

Sometimes on Saturdays there would be a spitting explosion from the oven and then Nanny would go over and open the door to emit a blast of succulent heat. The big roasting dish would be lifted out with a damp towel and the meat basted, and if the bones were done they would be picked up with a long fork and left to cool in a dish on the scrubbed deal table. They were the bones removed by the butcher before he rolled the beef and they were never taken to Nanny's home. If there were only two, one went to me and the other to Barry, but if there were three Nanny had one too and we would all pull up our chairs to the range and bite blissfully into the shreds of crispy meat. Nanny having no teeth just sucked away at hers and sometimes this was the story-telling stage. Occasionally she would tell us a conventional fairytale we knew already, but more often it would be a long rigmarole about, perhaps, a fox hunt and the various efforts of the fox to outwit his pursuers.

The details of these stories have, alas, all vanished from my mind and so have the fragments of rhyme with which Nanny enlivened the narrative. One line only remains: 'A bitch and a dog hanging.' Disembodied as the smile of the Cheshire Cat, it haunted me for years after we let Nanny go and finally lost track of her. I told it once to Aunt Harry and she was shocked. 'Just as well,' she told my mother, 'that Mrs Sheeran had to give up work if that was the sort of language she taught Barry and Emily.'

What sort of language? It had been the exciting culmination of a good story about a mean man who tried to cut his sons out of his will – was that it? Anyway, to open the door of his outhouse one day and find a bitch and a dog hanging from a pair of ropes (horrible grins on their dead faces) had been a sign of ill luck for that miserly man. A bitch and a dog hanging .... they hung still, after all these years, grinning in the cobwebs of the outhouse. Sometimes Nanny's stories were grim like this, and certainly they had none of the cosiness of Beatrix Potter or anything like that, but you never had bad dreams because of them. They were all part of stripping delicious crispy meat off warm bones by the fireside, of lashing rain outside maybe and the boundless comfort of Nanny within. She knew what to do for toothache and earache and how to stop soap from stinging your eyes:

she just breathed on a soft corner of the towel and laid it at once against the aching eye which instantly felt better. She knew how to evade telling the truth to enquiring parents who came home one day when Barry and I had been obstinate and rowdy and Nanny had refused to tell any stories. She never on this or any other occasion made complaints. On the contrary, if she came in to work on a day when we were already in trouble she would smooth things over and miraculously make peace. 'Sure weren't we young once like them ourselves ma'am, God be with the days we'll never see again.'

Nobody we knew, except my grandfather, owned a car, certainly not my parents. But when they would come home from the theatre in the rain, happy and full of chat, my father would add an extra layer of heavy brown paper to the parcelled meat and insist on carrying it for Nanny to the bus stop half a mile away. Sometimes, as we all knew, Nanny would be met at the other end by P.J., her eldest son, carrying a bicycle lamp. That would be on P.J.'s good days. Sometimes he had bad days when he would fall foaming on the floor of the farmhouse and Nanny would have to rush to get a spoon between his teeth. I found it hard to associate this damaged stranger with the quiet red-faced fellow in a cloth cap that I knew well and was a little afraid of. Sometimes during that unforgotten summer holiday he would come up soundlessly behind the swing his father had made and push me far away into the highest branches, which smelt of evening even in the middle of the day. I would swing down and twist my head to see P.J. grinning under his cap before he ran to send me up again out of reach. He hardly ever spoke and he hadn't attended school since the age of ten when one of the Christian Brothers had hit him with a pointer on the side of the head and he had fallen to strike the other temple against the desk opposite.

One day I strolled into the farmhouse kitchen to find P.J. a huddle on the stone flags in front of the fire covered by a

dark blanket like the one on our swing, and hovered over
by Nanny who hunted me away sharply for the one and
only time I ever remember. When I saw P.J. again he was
just as usual, vaguely smiling and quiet and red-faced,
feeding the hens in the yard for his mother. He didn't mind
doing women's work. Some of his brothers laughed at him
for it. It was over P.J. that I saw Nanny angry with my
mother for the first and only time, and the sad thing was
that she was coming towards the end of her work for us
anyway. Why?

Forcing my memory, I am sure that some time around the
beginning of the '39 war my father's job became even more
precarious because the gas ovens and other equipment
couldn't be imported any more. My school kept me on at
reduced fees and the Saturday visits to the theatre (which as
we grew older we sometimes shared) stopped. Barry and I
were big enough now to look after ourselves. Fergus was ten
and my mother was learning of necessity to do her own housework. There came the embarrassed day when Nanny
Sheeran had to be told that we couldn't afford to keep her
on any longer, though my mother hoped she would drop in
for tea as often as she was near the house. Wouldn't she?
Nanny's already watery eyes filled up with tears and she
said of course she would and the childer (the old plural is
known to me only because of her) would surely run in and
out to her place now that they were bigger and had bicycles?
But before she left us my mother – who always had to be
meddlesome if she felt it was for somebody else's good – had
a word with Nanny about P.J. I was supposed to be doing
my homework at the kitchen table and I heard it all.

My mother said she knew how fond Nanny was of P.J.
and what a good fellow he was. But surely she should let
him go to the specialist place that was willing to take him,
now that they all knew he would never be better but certainly worse as time went on. Hadn't the doctor warned her
he might at some future date be dangerous, even to Nanny
herself?

'If he did itself, ma'am, God spoke before him,' Nanny said coldly. 'Sheeran and me will never part with our own flesh and blood to strangers, no matter what happens.'

What had become of them all? Christmas cards were exchanged for a while and we heard that the old house fell to a raw new corporation housing estate at the end of the war. The corporation built a new bungalow for the Sheerans in compensation, but how could you compensate for the way of life they had lost for ever? I vaguely remember the bungalow, modern and garish and full of ghastly new furniture to replace the settle by the fire and the wooden benches and the scrubbed deal table on which Nanny used to roll dough which she baked on the griddle over the open fire.

I could have found my way blindfold to the old farmhouse, but the exact whereabouts of the bungalow I had forgotten. Anyhow the housing estate which filled the fields I had known was now a quite elderly suburb, with beyond it new and even uglier acres of housing. You could drive five miles from where Mick Sheeran had put up the swing for us and not see a field or a tree anywhere. Somewhere in this wilderness of concrete, however, great-grandchildren of Nanny's and Mick Sheeran's were probably playing and there was nothing to tell me which children. I left the car and went wandering through the little streets, each called by the name of an Irish clan. A group of lounging boys in high boots consulted silently together when I asked them if they knew of a bungalow tucked away somewhere here among the houses. It was a small child several groups later however who pointed up a laneway between the houses before running away with her skipping rope. I fancied she crinkled up her small eyes the way Nanny used to do.

And she was right about the bungalow. There it was where I should have remembered it, standing forlornly in a small vacant lot that was surrounded by the untidy back gardens of the other houses. Its own garden was bosky and overgrown; it was a long time since the front had seen any paint.

Something about the large pale middle-aged woman who opened the door reminded me of the Sheerans' youngest daughter whom I had known as a slender giggling girl working in a jam factory. Rosaleen? When I announced my own name she let me in. Rosaleen it was. Her husband was at Croke Park and her children were all out – she had been just going to lie down for a while. When I asked for her mother she looked a little defensive.

'Alive and well thank God, ma'am, and living in St Kevin's – I wasn't strong enough to look after her now that her eyes are so bad.'

'And your father?' I said.

'Dead and buried this twenty years,' the large woman said. 'He never did a day's good after we left the old house.'

'I can hardly believe he's dead. He used to swing me up to the birds long ago. Not as high as P.J. did, though. How is P.J.?'

'Not a bother on him. Easier than any of us. He got too much for us all and we had to sign him in one day when she wasn't here herself. She never knew it till she came home from Tommy's place and found him gone. He's better off where he is, that's what we all say, but of course she broke her heart over him. . . .'

'Of course. Could I call to see your mother some time?'

I wanted to show Nanny our daughter Sarah. I wanted to watch her pondering resemblances between the small wilful golden creature and my dead parents.

'Visiting between two and four Sundays and Wednesdays,' Rosaleen said. 'I'd be much obliged to you for visiting her, ma'am, because it's a long trek over from here. I try to go every second Sunday if I'm not too tired.'

I refused the cup of tea that she offered me with all the courtesy of Nanny herself and let her go to her rest. Some day I might visit St Kevin's. But not today, although it was Sunday. Some day I might say to her: 'Tell me how you and Sheeran lived happily together all those years of endless work for other people. Tell me how you reared six or seven children and still had grace to spare on less money per week than Sarah has now for pocket money. Tell me.'

Before I reached the city centre I knew I wasn't confident enough or generous enough or brave enough ever to see Nanny again. If she couldn't tell me it was all true, if she could no longer charm away the pain from my eyes how could I live and bear it?

Four Green Fields

THE house seemed empty when they got in from the road, but Denis made a quick tour of the upstairs rooms just in case his wife might be getting ready to go out. The American girl, in pink and white gingham, tagged along behind.

'Sometimes I dream of this house,' she said. 'And then I smell apples and hear the pigeons make their clamour in that tree out there. Like the first time I came. Like every time.'

'Not this pigeon,' Denis said. He stood transfixed in the door of the room with a sudden feeling of horror he couldn't explain. His guest stood behind him as though in a bus queue. On the bed near the open window was a young pinkish bird with folded wings and head buried in the tufted white cotton of the bedspread. It lay as though floating head downwards on water.

'Asleep,' Mary Kate said, amazed, following him across the room. 'Asleep like a person on a bed.'

'Dead like a person on a bed,' Denis corrected. There was no blood anywhere, not even when the girl lifted up the plump warm body in her hands. But on the mantelpiece among blue glass floats and chunks of rock and a photograph of Sarah at school there were a few feathers slightly blood-stained at the tips. The blood was already dry. Man and girl walked from the mantelpiece to the open window and back again to the warm hollow on the fluffy cotton where the bird had lain.

'A hawk?' Mary Kate guessed.

'In inner suburbia? I hardly think so. But I think this was an inexpert flyer who misjudged the open window. He probably hit the mantelpiece with some force and all the damage happened under the feathers. He was half stunned, and could fly no further than the bed.'

'So he died tidily on it,' the girl said. 'So goddamn tidily.' Rocking the body of the pigeon in her arms she began to laugh wildly so that her companion couldn't be sure at what point the laughter dissolved. 'Last year they pumped me for three hours in hospital when all I wanted was to die tidily like this one.'

'That was last year,' Denis said firmly, taking the dead bird from her with hands that were still shaking. 'You are a year older and much more sensible and your good thesis on John Millington Synge is entirely prepared and already half written. You're going to be all *right*. Come downstairs and I'll make you some coffee. Come on.' But first he remembered to pick the few feathers off the carpet where they had drifted, and he remembered to search till he found a single dried spot of blood on the white mantelpiece which he wiped away. He didn't want to trouble Emily with any traces.

In the kitchen was the old cat, eager for company, and a note from Emily. Mary Kate read it aloud as her host disposed of the dead bird in the incinerator.

'Think I'll go straight on from town to O'Sullivan's where they plan to eat early (seven-thirty for eight o'clock, remember?). Will you follow on when you get back – they'll be disappointed if you miss it. Love. E.

'P.S. Hope Mary Kate met her father all right and that you aren't too tired after the long drive back. Liver for the cat in the fridge – can you believeit ? E.'

'What will she say Denis? I can't just *be* here when you both get back.'

'You'll come with me to the party, that's what you'll do. I'll phone to fix it with Siobhán O'Sullivan. It's an open sort of house anyway. We haven't seen them since we got back from holidays so it's certain to be a cheerful evening.'

'But what will Emily *say* when she hears I ran away from my father and back to here again?'

'She'll most likely tell you Sarah's room is free and you can stay here till you decide when you do want to go to the west.'

'But Denis, do *you* even understand? I couldn't go up to him at Shannon because I saw whiskey in his hand and when he drinks – which he probably did because he had to face seeing me after two years and a new wife I've never seen – he goes on and on and on and it can last for weeks. . . .'

'Stop thinking about it now. I'll make you coffee after I've fed the cat. Why don't you go out and air yourself in the garden? Emily has a seat in the sun out there – look.'

As he stooped to pick up his ragged cat, the girl stooped too and kissed the back of his neck. 'Run out like a good child and I'll bring you coffee out there,' Denis said smoothly, and because her gesture had been totally ignored the girl obeyed, shaking her head baffled as she went. The clock up in the hall struck the hour. Half past five. The garden was loud with birdsong.

Town was sultry and grey and Emily had a message to do for an elderly relative which took her all over the city and finally to a part of it she seldom saw these days. Talbot Street used to be 'town' when she was a child, always crammed on Friday with large female shoppers who butted children in the face with full shopping bags and never apologised. The way to pass relatively unharmed was to hold your head up and keep your eyes fixed on Nelson on top of his pillar. That way you might sustain bruised elbows or sore ribs but your face had a chance of remaining un-damaged. That way also you had a chance of losing your mother which was a terrifying thing when it happened.

What you did then was stay exactly where you were until she found you. That was the rule. You didn't look for her or you were lost indeed. Emily had a vague memory of such an occasion and of subsequent comforting in Bewley's on the other side of O'Connell Bridge but visits to Bewley's were expensive and mainly connected with Christmas or the annual pilgrimage to buy school shoes in Bradley's.

Talbot Street was now both brighter and shabbier than it used to be, full of boutiques blaring pop music and selling trendy gear of American origin, T-shirts stamped with declarations of one sort or another, denim garments of every kind including underwear. Older establishments selling furniture or books or matrons' drapery had grown dimmer and shabbier, brick fronts no longer cleaned or pointed, awaiting the moment when the owners would sell out and the shopfront be adorned with yet another paper banner announcing another boutique or another cheap Indian bazaar. The general seediness reminded her of the one place in the known world she had found dismaying, Praed Street in London, where faint painted medallions on the crumbling brick proclaimed 'Surgical and sexual appliances a speciality'.

She doubted if even in Praed Street the piece of apparel formerly known as a 'modesty vest' could be found. The elderly relative had been specific however about the places in Dublin likely to stock this garment of her youth but she had been proved wrong. Merry's of Talbot Street had been suggested by a friend of Emily's. Crossing the street to the shop at the traffic lights, she was beside a young family setting out apparently for a late afternoon stroll in Stephen's Green. A flaxen-haired toddler carried in one hand a crumpled brown paper bag whose contents Emily could guess. The other hand was held by the child's father who looked as if he ought to be still at school. The ducks, he was saying, might be well fed by now since it was getting a bit late in the day, but the seagulls were greedy buggers and could always put away more grub. The child said she didn't want to feed the seagulls. Her equally young mother pushed

a go-car with a smaller child fallen asleep sideways on a pink
pillow. Just before they reached the pavement where there
was a parked car, the long-haired girl glanced back to check
that her family hadn't been cut off by a change of lights, and
then quite suddenly the world exploded all around them in
flames and noise and falling mortar. Emily seemed to be
looking down from a great height through clouds of smoke
at bodies with open mouths from which no sound came.

This story, like two or three very similar ones, would last
Feardorcha O'Briain all night. He was a senior counsel who
took mostly Provo briefs these days. His story would be
abandoned several times in the course of the meal and taken
up again if a gap presented itself in the conversation. It was
long and dull and concerned details of the Coventry bombing
in 1940. Very often it sidetracked back to 1916. Sometimes
he interrupted the story himself with verses from a newish
ballad of which he approved. He had the remains of a good
parlour voice.

> ' "What did I have?" said the fine old woman,
> "What did I have?" this fine old woman would say,
> "I had four green fields and each one was a jewel
> But strangers came and tried to take them from me." '

A young American couple researching a book on the
influence of revolutionary history on Anglo-Irish literature
had heard most of the Coventry story before and tomorrow
after breakfast in Percy Place they would go over their notes
yet again with a bright red marker indicating cross references.
    'Siobhán, a chroí, won't you send Emily over to me as
soon as she arrives, till I see would she remember whether it
was the Da or Jimmy Mallon took the rise out of the camp
commander that time on armistice night? Virginia here is
very particular about the details, aren't you, my treasure?'
    Virginia O'Hagan was adept at avoiding the large en-
circling hand but smiled pacifically at him and nodded her

head. She had already noted the bottle of whiskey stashed away against the wall. These times he didn't travel without adequate personal supplies, she had been told.

'Yes, a tincture if you please, Brian, and would you switch on the news till we see what way the world is at all at all?'

'Siobhán wants us to sit down and eat very soon – is it worth while?'

'You'd never know, you'd never know what you might miss, maybe a particularly important commercial,' O'Briain said.

'Well anyhow Denis and Emily haven't got here yet,' the host agreed, switching on the television set. A panel game was nearing its end but after a couple of seconds there was a news flash.

Details are becoming clearer about this afternoon's car bomb explosion in Dublin's Talbot Street. It has been established that at least twenty people have been killed outright and dozens injured, some of them seriously. Emergency services are in operation. A full report will follow the Nuacht at eight o'clock.

Outside in the hall the phone was ringing above the shocked clamour of the guests and Brian went to answer it. 'Yes, yes of course. Bring her and welcome – no problem. Have you heard the shocking news?'

He gave it briefly and noted the long gasp from Denis at the other end before he asked whether Emily had arrived yet. She was to have come straight on from town. 'No, Denis, she's not here yet, but it's much too early to get worried. Town must be in chaos because of the bombing – you can imagine the traffic jams. Come over at once and we'll all worry together.'

The host dodged briefly back into the kitchen to tell his wife Siobhán who covered her eyes in horror and began to gibber about Emily. She most probably had been in Talbot Street that afternoon because Siobhán herself had suggested

Merry's as a possible place to find some outmoded garment for the old aunt. And then suddenly the doorbell rang and there was Emily in the porch, white-faced, bloodstained, filthy, but unquestionably alive and begging a pound to pay for her taxi. It was unlikely, Emily said, she'd ever see her handbag again. And then almost immediately her husband was rushing up the path to clasp her in disbelief.

'No panic,' he said. 'I've paid off your man. O, Emily.'

They were laughing then and embracing like lovers. Emily was apologising for not phoning at once – there were queues a mile long at all the phone boxes. Into the hall edged the girl in pink gingham to join the groups of friends waiting until their presence was noticed. The girl's presence had however been noted by Emily in a quick exasperated smile.

'Tell you the story later, Emily,' her husband said in her ear. 'She ran like a redshank from her father so I suppose we'll have to put her up for a few days.'

'Fine, she can have Sarah's room,' Emily said.

'I lapped up superstition with my mother's milk, did you know that?' Denis was saying. 'And I haven't drawn an easy breath since I found a dead pigeon on our bed this afternoon.'

'How apposite the knave was,' Emily quipped. 'A witty bird, if dead itself.'

'You're not dead anyhow.' He hugged her again and they turned to face the impatient people in the hall, both of them embarrassed by their self-absorption.

'I'm sorry to be late and glad to be alive,' Emily smiled, and then the questions rained on her. 'No, no, I was thrown clear,' she said. 'All I have is a bruised elbow where I was flung against a hotel railings. Look, that's all. But the first three people I tried to help turned out not to need it – not ever again. And two babies on their way to feed the ducks in Stephen's Green, as Sarah used to do, were blown into fragments. One moment the one who could walk was talking to her father and carrying her paper bag of bread, and the next moment she wasn't there any more and I never saw her again. But I saw them carrying her father away on a stretcher with something clutched tight in his hand – the baby's hand, I think. I saw so many people being gathered into plastic bags.'

Emily began to shiver violently and was taken away to a warm bath by her hosts. When she appeared half an hour later she was calm and clean, with wet hair, arrayed in one of Siobhán's long cottons which was too big for her. Feardorcha O'Briain made a cavalier bow to her, removed his tie and offered it to her as a belt. The Americans noted that he must have been handsome once and very like Michael Collins. Emily fastened the tie on and they all sat down. O'Briain was unsteady but didn't seem drunker than usual.

The host thought their food would be attacked with raging appetites but nobody except O'Briain ate much. It wasn't until the coffee stage had been reached that they realised just how drunk he was. Almost a full bottle of wine had been added to his day's quota and now when the host unwisely passed around the brandy, O'Briain poured it for himself as though it were wine. He had been making no more of a nuisance of himself to his immediate neighbours than usual until somebody mentioned the bombing again and then he staggered to his feet as though addressing a public meeting, raised his glass and shouted: 'I give you the beginning of the end, friends. Every bomb that shatters capitalist complacency in the south brings us nearer to the day when there will be a final withdrawal of enemy troops from Ireland. When that day dawns north and south will be united in bloodshed – Christ knows nothing was ever achieved without bloodshed in the history of this unfortunate island. After Ireland's second Civil War there will be an end to the effects of seven hundred years of foreign domination. We have to bring the fight down here into the south by any and every means in our power because there is no other way to the ultimate aim of a United Irish Socialist Republic.'

'Is bombing babies in prams north and south a permissible means to this end?' That was Emily, white-faced again.

'Regrettable but inevitable, my treasure.' The eyes were

mad and bloodshot now but his articulation was profession-
ally perfect. 'You won't have forgotten that a prematurely
senile politician said six years ago that we wouldn't stand
idly by and watch our people in the north tortured and
beaten back into the ground by the forces of imperialism?
But by the sweet suffering Jesus we did stand idly by and
we'll go on doing it whatever fucking lot of power-drunk
gombeen men are in power in Dáil Éireann until we are
made to see that the crisis is not the north's problem but
ours, the concern of all of us, and that the only way forward
is total reshaping of our society after a civil war that is, any
way, inevitable. It's not and it never was "a little local
difficulty" as that imbecile Eden said about Suez. It's the
finish of the job that was begun in blood at Easter sixty years
ago, and won't end until the Brits get out and the streets of
every town in the south run redder with blood than the
streets of Belfast will tonight.'

Unstoppable now, he rounded suddenly on the Americans.
'What we want from you, friends, is money and guns, not
theses. Fuck the half-baked phoney talk of John Millington
Synge that obsesses you and his sorry dozens of imitators.
The landowning classes like your William Butler Yeats and
George Moore and Augusta Gregory made a career for
themselves out of the craven quaintness of a poverty-
stricken tenantry. We want no more patronising Anglo-Irish
geniuses and no more quaint peasants or urban slaves. I
regret as much as the next man the death of children and
civilians that is a necessary adjunct of urban guerilla warfare
all over the world. We have to end suffering by temporarily
making more of it – we have to. . . .'

The big drunken historic ruin of a man stopped abruptly
as the American couple with a gentle touch on the shoulders
of their hosts left the room. Emily followed, glad that somebody had taken the initiative, and somebody else at the
table poured more coffee for O'Briain and pulled him back
into his chair. He deliberately took up the cup and poured
it over the tablecloth before staggering to his feet and up the

stairs. The host followed with Denis who offered to drive O'Briain home. Nobody would be sorrier or quicker to phone with his apologies in the morning than the same parlatic madman, Denis said.

In the next room Emily switched on the television for the late news, and the little huddle of people around her heard more reports of deaths in the city casualty wards. Also two Catholics had been shot dead in a village pub in Armagh and four Protestants seriously injured when masked raiders sprayed a Sandy Row lounge with machine-gun fire. A member of the Westminster opposition had been slightly injured in a car bomb explosion outside his Mayfair flat, and news had just come through of the death in mysterious circumstances of an Irish student in Paris.

Meanwhile outside in the hall were the sounds of O'Briain's departure. His hosts held him upright while Denis brought around the car and he continued in a maudlin bellow to lament the fourth green field of the proud old woman whose sons had sons brave as were their fathers. Emily sat listening among the friends who remained.

'When I was ten,' she said, shivering, 'I had that man's picture pinned up on my wall at home. With Pearse and Dev and Yeats and Bold Robert Emmet.'

Loser

ON the last day of his life Dan decided that the women who
haunted you were not those whom you had enjoyed or even
known remotely well, but strangers who had at one time or
another troubled you with the most transient flicker of
desire. He hadn't a face for most of them. One was repre-
sented by a pair of crossed ankles on the Dalkey tram,
another by a smile which had temporarily blotted out the
entrance of Mitchell's where he was going to meet a friend,
another was remembered only by a laugh or a gasp of greeting
or a pair of chubby breasts bare below him in the parterre
when fashion had newly decreed flattening and covering.
He was troubled by all the women in turn, all over again,
as he rocked along by tram after Fairyhouse to visit his sister
in Ballsbridge. It was no use anyhow planning how he would
approach her for money. That was something you had to
play by ear every time. Now that poor Mother is dead you
are my only refuge. No. That failed last time. Play the thing
by ear. As he knew.

She was tinkering as usual in the garden and didn't look
pleased to see him. He kissed her playfully, then lifted up
the hand which was not carrying a flowerpot and searched
for green fingers.

'No use. You may as well leave the cuttings alone, sister
Harriet. Your fingers are shelly pink and much too pretty.
Come in and brew your famished relative the pot of tea he's
been dreaming of. Look, I brought you meringues from
Mitchell's.' Smiling he held up the blue and white box and

then she had to smile too.

'Oh very well. At all events I was nearly finished.'

Sparrows chattered among the ivy that lined her front walls, and the spring breeze had a touch of the sea in it. She would have preferred to remain out of doors. But there, even now as a wife she was at the beck and call of her brothers and sisters just like long ago at home. He saw the complaint in her face and set about amusing her in the spotless tiled kitchen that yet seemed dark after the spring light outside. A canary in a domed wicker cage sang shrilly at the open window. There were geranium pots on the deeply recessed ledge, a few of them overflowing already with new growth.

'So Medway was too bally lazy to see to it himself and left the booking once again to yours truly. It's true I approached the Carl Rosa for the same week but I didn't finalise the arrangements. Medway did that and then forgot to put it in the book. He says he discussed it fully with me to the last detail but I've no recollection of it. It can't be denied that I could have been a wee bit the worse for wear after Leopardstown but the fact remains it should have gone down in the book. Failing to write it up was the root of that particular little problem.'

'What little problem?'

He laughed merrily like a beloved younger brother and complimented her on the tea. 'Oh, but wait until you hear! Dear Noel himself couldn't have done better.' He jumped up and put on the soft black hat again, this time at a rakish angle over the untrustworthy china blue eyes. He settled one shoulder against the fireplace and struck an attitude.

'Here am I, sister mine, in the absence of Medway entertaining the manager of the Carl Rosa to coffee in the top office with a choice selection of his stars. It's only eleven o'clock in the morning and rehearsals start in half an hour and will go on all day. Their men are helping ours to clear the dress circle bar for the Tosca rehearsals – they'll open with Tosca next week. Everything in the garden is rosy.' He swept off the hat and bowed, kissing imaginary hands.

'Compliments have been exchanged all round. The stars are delighted with their suites in the Shelbourne. Ireland is a charming country, devoted to grand opera. Best audiences in the British Isles. All that sort of thing. Your little brother is feeling sanguine at the prospect of a good season and Medway's praise (with a practical expression of it perhaps in next month's cheque) when Stan comes in with that agitated expression on his beery old face. "Mr Montgomery, sir, I'm sorry to butt in. Gentleman downstairs says he must see you. Shocking urgent, sir. Gentleman from Moody Manners, sir."

'Stan has only finished this rigmarole and light is suddenly and horribly beginning to dawn on yours truly when a very large gentleman in a bowler hat explodes into the office. Language most unfit for the ears of ladies – horrible. Consternation at happy coffee ceremony. Somebody spills a scalding cup on somebody else's foot and dear Dolly starts to scream from sheer nerves. It's the contralto's foot not Dolly's which is scalded but *she* is stunned into silence. Shocking scene.'

'But what was it all about?' Harriet felt she ought to be able to interpret her brother by now but this scene defeated her.

'Dear old girl – patience. You shall hear. Picture the annoyance of the manager of a well known opera company when he arrives with his little band at the North Wall and there's nobody to meet them. Irish courtesy and hospitality and all that. Not a sign of it. He takes a taxi to the theatre and what does he find?'

'Dear goodness!' Harriet understood at last. 'Oh, Baby, how could you?'

That was a good sign. Calling him Baby was a good sign. Dear little chap that she had dandled on her knee and cared for like a mother.

'Not my fault, ducky. Reflect. There's nothing in the book – no record of the booking. No way I could have understood that I was booking in the Carl Rosa for a fortnight

already agreed on with Moody Manners. Medway's Method
was at fault – nothing whatsoever to do with yours truly.
But who must take the knock? Whose career is in ruins at
this moment? Not Medway's, I assure you.'

'Come and sit down, Baby, and drink your tea. These
meringues are delicious. Have another. I'll warm up that
cup for you. There must be something you can do.'

This was the cue he had been waiting for, and he sat down
heavily again in front of the geraniums, head in his hands.
'Have you any remote conception of what this means to
me?' he said brokenly. 'They were at first claiming all their
costs and also damages. Now Medway has softened up the
manager to the extent that he will accept return travel costs
with a firm booking for May on much better terms.'

'Isn't that splendid? Cheer up now, Dan, like a good boy,
and stop breaking your heart over it.'

'Travel costs to be recovered from *me*, Harriet. From *me*
who haven't a penny in the wide world except my salary –
totally inadequate for some time now.'

'I'm sure you're being too gloomy about it, dear. Mr
Medway would never be so unreasonable.'

'Wouldn't he though? It's pay up or get out. As simple as
that. Theatre finances are tricky enough at the moment.'

'Wouldn't your bank accommodate you?'

'Not a chance!'

'Father then?'

'The old man has paid up a few small personal debts too
recently for me to ask so soon again. You are my only
hope.'

'I? You must be dreaming, Dan – several hundred pounds
might be involved?'

'Say an even thousand and everybody would be happy.
You'll be paid back of course, with interest.'

'I think you must be joking, Daniel. Richard and I simply
do not have on hand a huge sum like that.'

'Never mind Richard – you had more than that salted
away yourself before you married him.' It was a fact well

known in the family that she had the first halfpenny she ever earned.

'That's quite enough of that sort of talk. You're forgetting yourself as usual, Daniel – I never heard such a proposition in all my born days. If poor Mother could only hear you. . . .'

'If Mother was alive I wouldn't even have to ask. She'd do the offering – you know that!'

'Poor Mother was in a stronger position financially than I am. I'll have to ask you to excuse me – I must get back to the garden and finish before it's time to see to Richard's meal. In fact I'm late as it is. I'm truly sorry, Daniel.'

True to form he wasn't even Dan now, not to speak of Baby. He was Daniel, the same troublemaker he always was, a nuisance to the family even at school. Fancying himself a hero and joining Fianna Eireann and drilling out in Santry when he ought to have been at his books. A brave young soldier laddie until he was needed and then causing endless trouble to them all trying to escape his involvement. She remembered the white feather some Eccles Street girl had sent him and how lightly he had taken it. 'Take a trophy for your chapeau, sister mine. Somebody has kindly sent me a premature decoration.'

He was only a schoolboy but it was true they were all ashamed of him just the same. It was the time for heroic gestures. He had two brothers out in Flanders fighting for little Belgium. He had burned his Fianna uniform in the back garden and applied himself so well to his studies over the next six years that he was barely twenty-three when he was called to the bar. Amateur dramatics became his craze, however, and eventually took over from the law. Some small parts, a lot of luck, occasional professional chances with touring companies, brought him in due course to the position of house manager in the Gaiety Theatre with a safe progression to manager and a seat on the board on Mr Medway's forthcoming retirement. If only he would keep his nose clean. If only he would develop a belated sense of responsibility even now. But no. This sounded like his most serious piece of trouble to date.

'Dear Harriet, listen to me before you go back to your tulips. I need your help now as I've never needed it before. I implore you not to throw me to the lions.' He turned the full battery of his desperate charm on her and smiled the smile whose various stages she could remember from child to man.

'I'm truly sorry, Dan. You'll have to accept that I can't go on helping you for ever. It wouldn't be in your own ultimate interest even if I could.'

'Then goodbye, Harriet, and thanks for the tea. But remember I warned you that you won't like the pieces the lions leave behind.' On their way along to the side door, he put two fingers into his breast pocket and pulled out an envelope. 'I almost forgot. I brought you a couple of briefs for the show next week.'

'You never do hold grudges, do you? Bless you, Dan.'

'It's called style, darling, and it's much rarer than talent. Goodbye.'

Quite suddenly he was gone, banging the door behind him. She sat down on the bottom step of the stairs to cry, her garden forgotten at last.

Outside the cherry trees in all the front gardens gave off their acrid smell in the sunshine and Richard was coming with his shiny briefcase and rolled umbrella from the direction of Lansdowne Road. You poor vanquished bastard, Dicky. She'll suck you dry and polish up the remains and send you out a prosperous citizen with your briefcase every morning in good time for the eight-thirty and nobody will ever know that you're dead, that you died a dozen years ago.

'How's the form, Dan? You don't look your usual perky self I must say.'

'Come on over with me for a snifter before supper and I'll tell you all, Dicky.'

'Thanks for the offer but Harriet has something planned

for this evening. I promised her faithfully I'd be on time.' The pale blue eyes were apprehensive, yet looking longingly in the direction of Mooney's pub.

'It won't take us ten minutes. Come on, Dick. Be a devil for once. She's not ready for you anyway – I've just been there.'

It was cool and quiet in the pub. There was only a scattering of men drinking, but the snug door was half open showing a neat pair of ankles and high-heeled green shoes. Dan called for two small Jamesons. Then Richard ordered two large ones and listened with widened eyes to the highly coloured tale of the bungled bookings. Finally he laughed enviously.

'Never a dull moment, Dan. You'll never grow old like the rest of us. Would you believe I had a nice voice myself when I was a boy. Sang in the choir in Berkeley Road, did you know that? Might have made a name for myself if I'd got the chance. But my old man was always pushing me at the books – like your own father, I suppose – wanted me in the legal partnership, don't you know? Now that I have responsibilities I suppose it's just as well but sometimes, just sometimes, I wish. . . .'

He stared so distantly into his glass that Dan could have strangled him. Listen, you old fool. Understand.

'My responsibility at the moment, Dicky, is to cough up enough money to cover the company's losses. If I can do that, I'm away again. Old Medway is prepared to let bygones be bygones. But if I don't. . . .'

'Poor fellow,' Richard said, 'it's a difficult situation.' Suddenly Dan felt he had to tell somebody the truth. Even Dick Reidy.

'Listen, Dick, old skin, I very nearly made it today on a borrowed fifty quid. Two-thirty at Fairyhouse – my tip was a certainty at a hundred to one. Outsider called Fox Trot couldn't lose, the chappie said. So I'd made up my mind. Fifty for a win. Made up my *mind*, Dicky, you understand? But going in the gate I met the Nag Montague – remember him? Haunted the stables since he was a nipper. Said I was mad, misinformed. Fox Trot hadn't an earthly. The horse that was a certainty for the two-thirty was Bitter Sweet – the tip came from the trainer who knew the form of the whole field.'

Now it seemed at last Richard understood. Drink suspended, he gave Dan all his appalled attention.

'You changed your mind?'

'Changed my mind. Fox Trot won, Dicky. Fucking Fox Trot won the fucking race by three lengths.'

Richard looked uneasily around at the few other drinkers to make sure nobody could see his brother-in-law actually breaking down, actually blubbing like a woman. Now Richard knew all he wanted to do was to make his escape home to Harriet as quickly as possible. He should never have come to the pub with Dan in the first place.

'There, there, old man. Don't take it so much to heart. Nothing is ever as bad as it seems at first.' He would apologise first to Harriet before she attacked him for being late, maybe take her a bunch of daffodils from the corner shop. There were daffodils in the garden but she hated plucking them.

'This is worse, and can only get entirely hopeless if I can't lay hands on a thousand quid inside twenty-four hours.' But Dan was not blubbing any more. He had raised his voice and Richard looked uneasily in the direction of the snug door which was open now. A young woman with avid eyes was watching them. A young woman of a certain class drinking gin alone.

'Maybe you should go over to the northside and see Fanny – how about that?' Richard offered shakily. The prominent blue eyes of his brother-in-law took on an ugly glitter. Richard knew himself that even mentioning Fanny in relation to borrowing money was treacherous, and worse, silly.

'My sister Fanny would give me her last farthing and so would her husband. It's to be regretted that that's not where the money is to be found in this family.'

'You'll have to excuse me, Dan. Would you not have another drink before I rush off? As I told you before, Harriet has something arranged for this evening.'

'I will have another Jameson since you offer it.'

Rapidly draining his own glass, Richard ordered another for his brother-in-law, who had relapsed into gloom again. 'Good luck, old man. The situation might change entirely after you've slept on it. Mr Medway might even see his way. . . .'

The farewell monosyllable from his brother-in-law was not one Richard cared to remember. Dan always had been ugly in drink. He hurried into the sunshine in the direction of the flower shop just as the young woman in the snug emerged and moved quite close to Dan, shamelessly giving him the glad eye.

She was not, Dan decided, a gift from the gods, their parting gift. She was neither as young nor as pretty as her ankles but she looked clean enough and cheerful enough and suddenly she seemed to Dan to embody all the women who had ever momentarily stirred him. She could be put in even more agreeable form by the single pound he had left in his pockets. When she told him she lived in a top room in Holles Street, a cosy attic under the slates with a window looking at the stars, he knew they would take a cab there and that his final exit had been reasonably stage-managed by the gods. It wouldn't provoke spontaneous applause, but it would be an exit that could scarcely go unnoticed, even by his family.

France is so Phoney

It's only that first lunchtime I remember clearly. There were a few others while the wind lasted and it was better to eat indoors. They all I think ended much the same, though the details are forgotten. But that first day the sun went in almost comically on cue when we were coming up the steep track from the beach and then you realised the wind was quite cold as well as unpleasant: the mistral, that blows like a threat over the summer people for a few days and then is gone.

Unlike the French who like to keep their rooms dark, we had opened all the shutters that morning and so the apartment was full of the lost sun's heat, welcoming. It had a faint delicious smell of Gauloises and coffee and maybe the last onion soup some Frenchwoman had cooked in the kitchen. It had white walls and white carpets; the furniture was dark and Spanish-looking and there were contemporary paintings everywhere. One of them I remember was by Arthur Armstrong, redolent of rain and home. Coady who had lent us the place went to all the more exclusive previews and bought what he fancied at the right price before the herd got in.

Denis unwrapped his long stick of bread ('It's called a "grande", Emily, in case you are ever wondering what to ask for in the shops,') and fetched a bottle of Listel from the fridge. When I came back from my shower he was engrossed again in Midi Libre with the wine at his elbow and a piece nibbled off the bread in front of him. He didn't look up when I fetched cheese from the fridge, plates, glasses and a bowl of apricots. The window was a curved bay overlooking the sea which now looked choppy as along the west coast at home although it was still a patchwork of blues. Over the third glass of wine we began to talk inevitably of Sarah, to wonder if she might be lunching off identical fare in Paris, to wonder whether she was alone by choice or with the friends she could command anywhere. Companionably we talked on to the end of the wine, and then he asked for coffee.

'Later,' I said, not able to keep from smiling. I had slipped without knowing it into a sensual mood which belonged in essence to long ago when Sarah was small, before I had learned to be cautious and not to court rejection. He looked up alarmed from his newspaper. 'We are not in any hurry, are we?' I said.

Later . . . we are not in any hurry. The phrases themselves belonged to a sexual life he had clearly forgotten although I had not. At times I felt all I had to do was stage-manage everything a little better and we might be back there again. We were perhaps back there again. But his hand reached for the cigarettes and mine for the matches, because once again this was all I could do for him.

'Aren't you tired after your long swim? Would you not like me to concoct some of my special coffee brew?'

I shook my head, desperately sorry I had begun this. His brown face in the matchlight was worried, his eyes predictably evasive. He suggested if I wasn't tired we might go and look at the museum which had a quite famous Roman section. It obviously was no afternoon for the beach. Besides, even if it had been, more sun would be bad for us, he said.

We went to the museum.

It was an eighteenth century town mansion of beautiful proportions whose upper salons were furnished exactly as they would have been originally, complete with Aubusson carpets and old silken curtains. A thick journal bound with tooled leather was open on a davenport, sharpened quill ready beside it. You fancied that the nobleman who had travelled home in the silk-lined sedan chair we had seen in the hall might at any moment come in to record the doings of his day. His lady's harp glittered like gold in a corner of the room and it would have been easy to spend a whole day just browsing among the furniture and the dozen or more Vernets which lined one wall.

Denis however was bored by detail and irritated by the elderly voluble American couple who shared the place with us. He said all this could be found anywhere in France, for heaven's sake, a lot of it could be found in the Vendrons' château. What was special about this museum was the Roman section. So we hunted for that through passages with worn floors of honey-coloured stone, hollowed outside every door by feet that had hesitated before going in. Denis was annoyed to discover at last a plan of the house which we had overlooked because of the sedan chair in the hall. The Roman section was in the basement. I left him studying the plan and wandered down there myself. The stairs below hall level were of wood, shallow, worn, and lovely to descend. But the basement floors themselves were monastic looking, of rough stone tiles. There was nobody except a tall plump American in blue denims studying the Roman remains. He ambled across to me almost at once, his white tombstones flashing in the fleshy face. He was wearing open sandals, and his toe nails were long and dirty.

'Show ya something,' he said good-humouredly as though I had known him all my life, 'ancient gods had their problems too.' One finger between my shoulder-blades, he guided me to a small creamy marble Apollo about two feet high. The face under its scultpured curls was perfect and rather beautiful but time or some other vandal had removed a nipple, one finger from the outstretched hand, and all of the genitals except a single testicle.

'Whaddya know,' the soft mid-Western voice was saying. 'Leave a guy face the world wearing one nut, no more.'

This was where Denis entered the conversation. His rope-

soled shoes had made no noise coming in. 'For all you would
be able to understand, he might prefer to have his brain-
power unimpaired. Look at the head. No brain damage,
you see.'

The American, to give him his due, summed up the
situation in one flash of the handsome eyes from my left
hand to Denis's face. Murmuring agreement, he was suddenly not there any more. Denis and I collapsed in laughter.
I remember the rest of that afternoon as mainly harmonious.
Despite a high-rise housing development outside the town,
the centre was intact and mostly medieval, narrow cobbled
lanes with washing strung across them, balconies full of
babies and gossiping women. The main streets however
were eighteenth century like the museum, broad and
beautiful with fountains playing among the shrubs of the
traffic islands. It was a town which had grown up around its
ancient university, some of whose schools were older than
those of the Sorbonne. It had a theatre and a concert hall and
a large population of apparently contented fully-integrated
coloured students. In the main square café where we stopped
they chattered in voluble French all around us – Algerians,
perhaps?

'I never thought I'd come to France again after Algeria,'
Denis said, frowning.

'On that reckoning one could never go to Portugal or
Greece or Britain or Germany – most of the world in fact
would be out.' He nodded, unwilling for argument, and
played with the water they always served here with coffee.
Under the striped awning the persistent cool wind crept. It
wasn't really a day for sitting around.

'You don't know where the post office is,' he said suddenly.
'You should know.'

'Have they stopped delivering mail in France?'

'It's a nice walk anyhow – I'll show you,' he pleaded.
'There's an alley full of cats on the way.'

We went walking again.

The alley full of cats had pots of geraniums too, standing

in the stone doorways, and again, overhead, the washing hung out to dry, clothes much newer and cleaner-looking than those of poor families at home. Denis tried to stroke his favourite kind of marmalade cat but the creature retreated in terror into a hallway which was full of children's voices. The next cat did the same but at last he cornered a grubby white kitten with one black ear and sore eyes.

'They aren't used to being fussed over,' I reminded him. 'Remember Françoise when she first came to us, how bored she was by the attention we paid to our cat?' We were off again on familiar ground, remembering. Denis stroked the kitten with gentle persistent hands until it began at last to purr. He wondered how lonely our Simpkin was. I wondered if Sarah's friend was remembering to come in and feed him every day as she had promised. We wondered if perhaps we should have sent the animal to stay with the local vet while we were away.

'Remember the year he escaped and ran home to an empty house when we were in Kerry?'

'Not ran,' Denis corrected, 'he made his way very slowly indeed. Remember we reckoned it took him ten days?'

'Yes, I remember. He always was a fool.'

Remember, remember. That was the year Denis had taken on Coady, fresh from college, and allowed him slowly to take over the office, handle all the major commissions himself, phase out the rest of the partners until (apart from the name) it was Coady's business, Coady's show. Ryan and Coady. More and more they were designing office blocks now, each, in my opinion, more hideous than the last. Georgian houses were falling one by one to the bulldozer, shadily acquired by the clients who got planning permission to rebuild even more shadily still. They applied again and again with donations to party funds timed to coincide with the latest appeal and eventually (however long it took) planning permission was granted even in areas scheduled for preservation. Ryan and Coady did what was regarded as a good stylish job, never cutting costs on popular touches like commissioned sculpture in the entrances or cotoneaster horizontalis in the patios behind. The clients invariably arranged for official openings at ministerial level which were noticed (with photographs) in the daily newspapers. More and more these days Denis was taking a back seat, refusing to make decisions, often electing to do site work which the most junior surveyor could have attended to without difficulty – the sort of work in fact which Sarah was doing now in her third year. All this could not be talked about so we discussed Simpkin instead.

· Denis sat down on the steps with the kitten cradled in his lap. 'Have you a tissue in your bag?' he asked me, and when I gave him one he tried to clean the cat's eyes, laughing when it suddenly lashed out at him before vanishing into the gloom. I offered him another tissue to deal with the blood but he shook his head and licked it away. The cathedral clock struck five.

At the post office the official summed Denis up impatiently as the man who had bothered her earlier.

'Rien du tout, monsieur.'

'Allez voir encore, s'il vous plait, madame.'

'Rien,' said the woman implacably.

Outside it was quite suddenly warmer and windless. Before we reached the fine Romanesque bridge its stone was golden in the late sun and in its shadow the eternal game of 'boules' was in progress. Elderly men in straw hats – worn always I was to learn in sun or cloud – poised and estimated and threw and argued over almost every shot. If you closed your eyes the hard pock of one metal ball against another, surprisingly like the sound of croquet, brought you back to the novels of Trollope and Thackeray. But that was in another country. Only the sound was the same.

I linked my arm through Denis's and led him under the bridge to the public park whose entrance was a miniature Arc de Triomphe. It was so warm I threw off my jacket and tried to part Denis from his but he hated to shed clothes. What you missed here was birdsong, he remarked, and he was right, of course. No birds sang. Instead there was the plash of fountains and children's voices in the labyrinth of little paths through the shrubberies, and everywhere of course the croaking of frogs. We climbed a stone plinth and walked between the legs of an equestrian bronze of Louis XIV, and then we looked down at the flower-pot roofs of the town, then at the spires of the cathedral we hadn't yet visited. Beyond it, far beyond, were hazy mountains and below us, to the left, the half-moon of the sea.

I should buy food, I thought idly, and as though he had heard, Denis said we'd eat out tonight. It would be a pleasant evening for strolling. Also there would be music in the park tonight – had I noticed the poster? I hadn't, of course. It was he who hardly looked yet noticed everything except my occasional moods of despair. I was astonished he should suggest eating out, he who hated any ceremony outside his own four walls. Now he seemed actually to be enjoying the prospect of dinner in town.

Long before the end of the meal I felt happy and hopeful. One always forgets how disappointing all holidays are in the beginning before some sort of ritual is established. From today it would be all right. I knew it as Denis ordered another bottle of rosé and indicated the label. 'Bouzique,' I read.

'It's situated on the salt lagoon of Sète,' he said. 'I'm going to take you there one day.' It sounded proprietary, like long ago. I'm going to take you there one day. As a student he had hitched over most of Europe whereas I had not. He wanted to show me everything he had seen, all the subjects of his bulging sketch books. We had not, in fact, travelled very much after Sarah was born.

'The village of Bouzique,' he went on, 'is chiefly known for the unusual way they have of catching shellfish. When we go you can watch it.' It was I who collected guide books, he who kept in his head every stray scrap of local information he had ever come across. 'You might even like to eat the wretched molluscs they catch.'

'Why not you too?'

'Food I endure,' he said, 'holiday food in particular. But I admit endurance becomes a positive pleasure where this wine is concerned.'

'Maybe we could take some home with us.'

'I don't think it would travel. Too light. The colour is curious. Colour of an onion skin.'

Here was the precision that had made him so good as a student. With a minimum of equipment he could have produced a working approximation to that exact shade in his sketches long ago. His mother once showed me a folio of them jealously preserved. The year he won the McKenzie Fellowship. His final year's win of an open competition for a concert hall in Dublin. The model for that was gathering dust in her dead drawing room. The plans for it were filed away for all eternity in the municipal offices of Dublin's City Hall. I asked him a question I wouldn't have dared to ask if we hadn't been half way through the second bottle of wine. He gave me one of his rare smiles of pure enjoyment.

'You've forgotten. I showed it to you once and you liked it. Think.'

What design that was ever really important to him had resulted in an actual building? Plans by the dozen I remembered. All of them had been altered or abandoned to his frequent despair. That was when he still cared.

'Doesn't the name Knocklacken mean anything to you?'

'That's the place you bypass on the road to Galway, isn't it? With terraced council houses all washed in different colours like the Kilkee seafront and a little main square with chestnut trees and a duck pond where the children play. Pines climbing up behind the houses. It isn't really like a council estate at all because ... I'm sorry. Oh God, I'm sorry Denis.'

He was broadly smiling now as he continued. 'It isn't really like a council housing estate because I didn't think of it that way. I thought of it as somewhere people would like to live. For God's sake, I fought even over those chestnut trees. They had to be chestnuts because of conkers in the autumn, you see.'

'I don't understand how I could have forgotten.'

'Don't worry, love, nobody else remembers either.' He spoke easily, completely without rancour. 'But since you asked me, it did give me pleasure to see it materialise exactly as I'd planned. It still does. There's a new generation of teenage parents growing up there who don't want to leave unless they can find somewhere like it. They can't because there isn't anywhere like it. It cost too much. It only happened at all because of the change of government at that time and an ambitious poor bastard of a minister who steamrolled Knocklacken through before anybody realised what he was doing. He's out of office now although his government is in again. An alcoholic, naturally. I see him sometimes in Neary's.'

Denis was laughing between sips of wine, as he often did when something distressed him. It was suddenly easy to talk to him, and I remembered with surprise all the times we could hardly exchange a word of any importance to either of us. He would talk to me about staff or cars; I would tell him neighbourhood gossip and there would be long silences before one of us mentioned Sarah. Then I would tell him her news – her friends' success at their exams or failure, affairs beginning or breaking up, the occasional shipwreck. But that night when the waiter brought coffee I felt I could have asked him anything, such as why he never wanted sex any more or why he didn't shoulder off Coady. Pay him off if necessary. I started with the second subject and his face closed slightly. Then he laughed, drank off the whole tiny cupful and ordered more.

'Je voudrais une tasse, s'il vous plait,' he said to the waiter with appropriate gestures, 'pas demi-tasse.'

'D'accord, monsieur. Et madame?'

'Ça va, merci.'

'All of a sudden,' said Denis, smiling across the table, 'you look like Mary Kate.'

Where in God's name was the sequence? I tried to stop my face from freezing and succeeded tolerably well, I think. I still had half a glass of wine left so I drank that slowly to buy time. But the question I wanted to suppress came out all the same.

'She is the reason why you keep fussing about the post, isn't she?'

'Sarah might some time be in some sort of trouble too, remember, and be glad of help from somebody like me.'

'She would phone you if she were. Why don't you answer me?'

'Mary Kate,' he articulated slowly, 'is a very frightened little girl who needs to be sorted out quite often. I'm a year or so older than her own father who isn't available. That's all there is in it, as you know perfectly well.'

Now I was beyond stopping myself though I knew how he would hate what I had to say. 'Even if her father were here she wouldn't want to go to bed with him. She obviously does with you.'

'Don't be silly. I sort her out, as I told you. She's sad and unstable and she knows her thesis will be terrible which doesn't help. She's not clever like Sarah and she's never had a proper home. You were sorry for her yourself when you asked her to stay, remember?'

'I never asked her to come back from California to stay again and again. I was merely obliging Dan O'Brien because he wrote that letter of introduction for her. You've let her assume disproportionate importance if you don't want to sleep with her.'

'Young girls, like flowers, are only at their best for a little while,' he said lightly. 'Everybody should enjoy being *à l'ombre des jeunes filles en fleurs* while the magic lasts. It's detached enjoyment, nothing to do with sex.' He was smiling again but it was clear his mind was miles away.

'Proust was talking about young men, in fact, but I suppose that's neither here nor there. If you were boss in your own company you wouldn't need such enjoyment,' I nagged on, hating myself now. 'Lucky Coady makes all the decisions (mostly wrong ones) and you never try to stop him. You sign agreements like a baby and then come home to write another long letter to Mary Kate. The business is going to ruins.'

'Let it,' he said lightly, 'I'm fond of ruins – I'm a sort of ruin myself.'

There were times when he looked like one but not always, not now. I put my hand on his in apology and suggested we walk back. Although I didn't entirely believe him about the American girl I wanted to believe him. It all seemed at that moment more than possibly true. Even more so during the stroll back hand in hand through the dusky yet brilliant gardens. It was Vivaldi this time and whole families idled together under the trees. The water which cascaded from the *châteaux d'eau* was bright blue and gold from invisible lighting below. A little band of Algerians played mouth organs and danced around one of the fountains.

> *'Allons dans les bois ma mignonette,*
> *Allons dans les bois du roi. . . .'*

Then another group we passed were singing a song by Moustaki: '*Non, je ne suis jamais seul avec ma solitude.*'

'France is so phoney,' Denis grinned, 'it's as though a stroll through the Phoenix Park actually yielded up leprechauns and crocks of gold. But it takes me in every time.'

'Me too. That's why I love it.'

The sweet solitude of the coast was phoney too, the lap of silky blue water against a deserted beach, a few sunshades still in position like sleeping butterflies. Nobody came here after seven, not even children as they would do at any Irish seaside resort. Here the older ones were at supervised summer camp in the mountains and the little ones had been tidied away out of sight by the Spanish au pair girls after an early supper. They were all asleep by now, probably. We climbed up to the verandah of the apartment by the beach.

No seabirds, of course. No sound but the lapping of water
and the distant drone of cars.

'I saw a Corot of this place once,' Denis said, as we stood
to look back. 'Not a very well-known or a very good Corot.
It was painted in July 1904 and this beach was as empty as
Mulrany. Not a house, not a parasol in sight. Half the canvas
was an evening sky just like that one. There was one beached
boat and a man walking near by with a dog at his heels.
That was all.'

'Where is this Corot?'

'I may have seen it in Paris – can't really remember. You
won't, I think, find it in any collection of prints.' We began
to talk without sequence about Paris when we first saw it
together, twenty years ago, but Denis inevitably went back
to his first solo hitching trip abroad, the year before he
graduated. All his real memories of places were of being
alone. Almost our only mutual memories for turning over
were of Sarah, always of Sarah.

'Would you like a nightcap,' he said unexpectedly when
we were inside.

'I'd love one.'

After he'd poured the drink he sat down on the white
carpet with a gesture of youth I hadn't seen for a long time.
The windows were open to the theatrical moonlight, and a
few summers ago I would have suggested a swim before
going to bed. Now I knew it would break whatever mood the
evening and the alcohol had built up between us. I couldn't
as yet speak for him but I knew I desired the relaxed yet
very slightly wary body as much as ever. He was smiling
and he hadn't put on the lamp which was a good sign. I
thought I wouldn't botch it this time so I made no move
towards him, just sipped the cognac slowly and smiled back
at him. Legs crossed in the strong reflected light, he looked
a little unearthly with the curly hair silver and everything
below it black, brows, lashes, eyes, beard. Like two cats we
sat watching one another for a long time. No sound but the
sea. Then he made some remark about Coady's taste in

booze and fearful lest the whole mood would collapse again like so many others I went and put my hand into his open shirt to feel the heartbeats. Instantly he recoiled like a snail whose horns have been touched, and then he leaned over to light the lamp while he continued his joke about Coady. I couldn't explain or control the sudden fountain of tears and he mopped at them patiently as though I were Sarah. I gained control quickly enough and found words I hoped would strike home.

'If I were not a little drunk I'd have known better than to try with lustful impetuosity for the third time in eighteen months. I'm so sorry.'

'I'm sorry too, Emily. But you should have known already how the idea fills me with revulsion – with you, with anybody. I've no hope that you will ever be able to regard this as a misfortune for me rather than an ingenious insult to you.'

'You prefer men then, like Proust?'

Even as I made the stupid taunt I knew how inappropriate it was. He laughed with genuine enjoyment.

'I almost wish I did.'

'So do I, Denis. So do I.'

I left him laughing in the bright lamplight and went down by the balcony and the steep steps to the beach. The air was warm and the wind hadn't returned. I had been walking furiously along the shoreline for twenty minutes before I realised I was walking not in the direction of a furled sunshade but of a man watching the sea. The red bead of his cigarette and the curling smoke about him gave him a touch of the bizarre. Not Corot but Robert Ballagh would have loved to paint him. Without any of the denim clothes in which I had seen him earlier that day in the museum I didn't recognise him at first (all fat men when naked look much the same) but then I remembered his soft mid-Western voice and then the handsome smoky eyes.

'I can recommend that water for a swim right now,' he said slowly, stubbing out the cigarette. 'I can recommend it because I've been in one time already. Come try it with me lady, unless your husband is following you like last time?'

For answer I wriggled quickly out of my two garments and ran with him into the water, thinking that after a second swim even his toe nails might be clean.

The Sisters

GOING by tram to the other side of the city was part of the treat. The child was usually quick enough to escape up the stairs when they got on at the Pillar and take her seat out in the front where you were always blown by the breeze and close to the exciting flashes of the wires overhead. Her mother, laughing though with exasperation, would follow her up the stairs and sit just inside the upper compartment with the door closed against the breeze but with a good view of all her daughter might be doing. When it rained, Emily would be called in, but she would always shout that it was only a few drops and would soon be over. Her mother couldn't hear her through the glass door but that didn't matter. If the rain were persistent Emily would be hauled in protesting that she would be sick inside, which she always pretended to be and sometimes was. Unless in the case of a positive downpour she usually had her way. She felt like a queen riding in a high carriage, ruler of everything spread beneath her: small people with short scurrying legs, men under the crowns of soft hats which appeared to be perched on faceless necks, cart-horses rattling over the cobbles, babies in prams small as the one Emily pushed into the hall of her doll's house. There were trees too and green lawns passing the railings to your left before you swung right at Elvery's where the elephant was. You could look into the elephant's small eyes which were about level with your own and feel at times that a stretched out hand could touch the tassels of his headgear. But stretching out your hand on the outside of the tram was strictly forbidden. There were fearful stories of electrocuted arms and hands knocked off as you passed lamp posts and if you broke the rules so flagrantly you could be brought in for good and angrily pinned to the seat inside.

There was a big green shop past Elvery's and it sold garden swings and lawnmowers and little white tables for having tea in the garden. That was what they sometimes had at Aunt Harry's. You went up a big flight of stone steps to Harry's hall door and so you had to go down a short flight of steps in the back hall and down more stone steps outside the back door to get into the garden. It was bigger than any other garden Emily knew, even her grandfather's, and it had pink brick walls and apple trees and a sundial but it had no swing. When she was let out there straight away she knew her mother and her aunt were going to talk about money. Once over tea in the garden Aunt Harry took her mother's hand before giving her a teacup and stared hard at the wedding ring. That was what Emily thought, anyway, but it wasn't at the wedding ring.

'So it's gone again?' Harry said, and her mother laughed uneasily.

'I'll probably be getting it out again at the end of the month when there should be some overtime.'

'What poor mother would have thought I daren't imagine. God spared her the knowledge of the mistake you made.'

This mistake was a frequent subject for comment by Harry. It had something to do with the size of the house they lived in and the small brother or sister that Emily had been told would be sharing her bedroom soon. Aunt Harry had a lot of dolls but no children in her house. It was bigger than any house Emily had ever been in. If her aunt offered to let her play with dolls in the bedroom she knew she must first say no, because her mother always signalled to her with her eyes. If she stayed, Aunt Harry often made jokes and fetched a big beach ball when tea was over, but if Emily went to play with the dolls she would see her mother's and aunt's heads wagging in disagreement when she looked down out of the big bedroom window beyond the laburnum tree.

'Like to play with the dolls, today, Emily love?'

'No thanks – unless I could bring the dolls down to the garden.'

'You know you can't do that, Emily. Fetch down the ball if you like from the hall chest.'

'All right.'

'Say "thank you," Emily.' That was her mother.

'All right, thank you.'

Sometimes even when she had been away for a short time because she ran all the way back, her mother would be blowing her nose or giggling uneasily when Emily came back.

'There is no need to discuss it any further. You know my views on the subject of borrowing,' Aunt Harry might be saying.

One day in winter after tea by the fire in the big front room, Emily's mother had shown signs of holding her own. 'I can easily check when I go home but I do think these *are* my teaspoons. Yours had no shell edging like these ones, Harry.'

'Nonsense, dear.'

'The ones mother gave you were the silver apostle spoons, I distinctly remember. The last time I used my silver spoons was at Christmas time when you and Richard came over on Stephen's night. You washed up for me, remember?'

'Very well, dear, I did take the spoons but only for safe keeping, knowing your careless ways. The next time it might be the spoons as *well* and where would you get the interest on both I should like to know? Of course you may have them back when things improve for dear Bartholomew if they ever do.'

'I *may* have them back if things improve!' Now to Emily's delight her mother was laughing, or rather giggling with the back of her hand against her mouth. 'Oh, Harry, you'll be the death of me yet!'

'You know I'm usually right, Fanny dear. You won't be tempted to do anything foolish if poor Mother's silver tea-spoons aren't under your hand.'

'Perhaps you're right. Would you like to take Mother's copper coal scuttle as well and the big blue dinner service and the Laughing Cavalier?'

'Those things are not so easily disposed of. Have another scone, Fanny dear.'

That evening when Uncle Richard came in with his brief case from the office, he drank a cup of tea quickly and then took Emily for a walk although it was so cold. He buttoned up her gaiters himself and wound a big scarf twice around her neck. They went down the Lansdowne Road to the Dodder.

'Why does Aunt Harry take the silver spoons away when she comes to our house, Uncle?'

'God bless my soul – what an idea, Emily! Where did you get this fancy from? Look at the robin over there and how he isn't afraid.'

'He can't see us.'

'Oh yes he can. They can see sideways. The eyes are at the side of their head, do you see?'

'Why does Aunt Harry sometimes make Mother cry? She never cries at home.'

'Don't walk too near the edge and I'll tell you a story. Once upon a time there were two princesses.' The river was noisy running over the stones. In summer you could see pinkeens but never in the winter. 'When the little princesses were children they played together and never quarrelled but when they grew up their mother died and the elder princess had to help the king to rule and keep everything going just as ever and then the sisters often quarrelled and the younger even hated the elder at times. But the people in the land were still happy because it was still ruled as well as when the queen was alive. Then the king died and the younger sister married the young prince they both loved but the elder sister who was queen now had to make do with an older prince who had a lot of money and wasn't very handsome. So they quarrelled more than ever whenever they met but they loved each other all the same.'

'What else?'

'Nothing else. That's the story. It's not very new and in fact it's as old as the hills – and if you don't like it you can always make up a better one yourself.'

'Daddy's stories are always more exciting. And funnier.' She knew she was being very rude but Richard didn't seem to mind.

'Does he tell you a story every night in bed?'

'Not every night. Not a story every night. Sometimes he tells me to close my eyes and we get on a train called the Slumberland Express. You can hear the steam getting up and the doors of the carriages rattling and children talking to one another and then the carriage doors banging and the guard blowing his whistle. And the train goes slowly at first then faster and faster and faster. . . .'

'And he makes all the noises himself?'

'When the train is really going fast you're asleep so you don't know. If I wanted to get off I couldn't. The next time I see him is shaving next morning. He puts soap on my face too. Then he goes off to work in the gas company. Where do you work?'

'In an office.'

'Is it your own office or somebody else's office?'

'My own office. Do you know what that is down there?'

'A heap of old newspapers and sticks and ice-cream packets and somebody's old shirt.'

'Wrong. It's a swan's nest. Next week or so you might see a swan sitting on it.'

'Can we come next week?'

'If Aunt Harry invites you, yes, and we'll go for a walk again, just the two of us.'

'Couldn't you invite me?'

'Yes, but I gave up doing that sort of thing years ago. It usually didn't work out, you see.'

The river path ended in a scatter of little houses with hens picking around them and up at the bridge the trams were turning round to go back into town with a lot of electric flashes against a lemon sky. When they got to the kiosk at the top of Pembroke Road he bought the *Evening Mail* final for himself and butterscotch for her in a white packet with C & B in gold along the edge, and the steps up to the house were steeper than when she arrived with her mother and one of them grazed her knee but it didn't hurt much.

After supper Richard took a bottle out of the sideboard and poured some for everybody but Aunt Harry tipped a little out of one glass and into Richard's before handing it to Emily's mother. Emily's glass had only a little port wine in the bottom and was filled up with warm water.

'Now Fanny, your health,' Richard smiled. 'And yours, Emmy.' The fire scorched her legs but the orange satin cushion with the silk tassels cooled them again.

'Have you been thinking over what we were talking about, Fanny?' Aunt Harry said, taking her port in tiny sips. Her smile was tight.

'Oh yes.'

'And what do you think, dear? Is it not a good idea, all things considered? I'm sure dear Bartholomew wouldn't stand in the way of a good sensible plan.'

'Yes, I'm afraid he would. He doesn't like the idea at all, you see.'

Emily knew it was one of those occasions when it was useless to ask questions, so she took a piece of butterscotch, carefully unwrapping it and tossing the rolled paper ball into the fire where it sizzled because it was greased paper.

'Won't you offer your packet around, Emily?' That was her mother. Apologising for having forgotten, Emily did that. They all thanked her.

'And why on earth would Bartholomew not think it a good idea seeing the way things are with no hope of improvement, rather the reverse?'

'He plans to organise a branch of the Workers' Union of

Ireland and campaign for better wages and stability, he says. The workers just need to be organised, you see.'

'I see that Bartholomew will end up without any job at all, like the last time he went to war. Typical of him to stir up trouble again instead of buckling down and getting all the overtime they can give him.'

'He says they should be paid higher rates for overtime, not the same.'

'He doesn't know his own luck in these hard times. Nothing will ever be the same again after '29. Doesn't he know that?'

'Why don't you discuss it with Mull himself?' It was clear now that Emily's mother was angry.

'I think,' said Richard, 'we should all drink up and even have a little more. Even get a bit tiddly. We'll talk about all this another time, eh, Harry?'

'No time like the present, especially when time is so short. Did you make everything quite clear to Bartholomew? That we would be responsible for education, clothing and all other expenses?'

'Yes, I did,' Emily's mother said. 'It's a generous offer. But you see we don't. . . .'

'You'll *see* E–M–I–L–Y very often, dear – it isn't as though we lived at the other end of the country. You will come to us and we will go over to you especially when the baby is too small to travel. Have no doubt about it, Fanny it's the ideal solution in your situation. The child is worth the best money can buy and you should know where money is shortest, just now and for a long time to come I'm afraid. Be sensible and unselfish like a dear good girl. I'm sure it's what poor Mother would have suggested if God had spared her.'

'Mother didn't part with any single one of eight children and I'm not going to either, so there!' Emily's mother blazed out at last and then immediately burst into tears. Richard fussed around her and Emily stood with one hand on her mother's knee. 'I think I'd like to go home,' she said.

'She'll be able to have music lessons, riding. . . .'

'We are s-s-saving up to buy a piano.'

'Your lawful debts must be disposed of first, I should imagine. She'll even be able to go to the university. Think of the future, Fanny.'

'That's enough, Harriet. You've said enough for one day. Let it be now.' That was Richard, always the peacemaker.

'I want to go home, please.'

'Very well, I've got something for you before you go, Emmy.' When Harry called her Emmy she always wanted something. 'Something you've always wanted, Emmy. Come till I show you, there's a little love.'

Her mother signalled to her to go, and the something was apparently in Harriet's bedroom. The place smelled of moth balls and eau de cologne and it was icy cold after the fire. But because of red chenille curtains and a red lampshade it looked warm. Harriet lifted down one of the rag dolls pinned to the red silk bell-pulls beside her mantelpiece. Turkey legs.

'Now love, that's for you to take home and keep.'

'No, thank you, that's the one with turkey legs.'

'Turkey legs?'

'They're sort of dead and bare like a turkey hanging up in the butcher's. I don't like them. Thank you very much but I don't want to take the doll home.'

'She was here before,' Harry said, sighing, when they went back to the drawing room. 'I don't know who she takes after but she was here before. Have a bar of Fry's cream chocolate then, Emmy, to eat on the tram.' Chocolate was stored in the oak and silver biscuit barrel on the sideboard.

'Thank you very much, Aunt Harry.'

Harriet waved to them from the top of the steps and Uncle Richard saw them to the tram. A cold wind whipped around the kiosk which was dark and closed up now. There were blue stars above the tram lines.

'Don't mind Harry,' Richard was saying, squeezing his sister-in-law's arm. 'You know the way she's always wanting to manage everything. You see she's so good at it, better than the rest of us put together. But if I had a whole houseful of children I wouldn't part with one either. I understand your attitude completely, Françoise.'

He had volunteered for France during the war and liked to remind people, her mother had told Emily, that he had learned to speak a little French. A tram came swaying along from Blackrock and he put half a crown into Emily's pocket.

'Don't be any more reckless than I'd be myself, Emily,' he smiled. Half a crown was unimaginable wealth.

'Thank you very much, Uncle Richard.' She kissed his cheek when he laid it against hers. It was thin and cold and smelled of shaving soap.

'Chin up, my love, and if you can't be good, be careful,' he said jauntily to Emily's mother as he handed her onto the boarding platform. He swung Emily up beside her and though she was too big for that sort of thing she didn't mind. Beside her on the platform was an advertisement which said LOBO, delicious sweets and chocolates, 9 Lower Baggot Street. Her mother hauled her firmly into the lower compartment.

'Can't we go up, can't we, to see the lights?'

'It's too cold up there at night-time. Wave to Uncle Richard, there's a good girl.'

They waved to Uncle Richard until he was a small speck surrounded by a blowing white scarf and he waved to them. Her mother held her tightly clasped as though she were a baby again. The tram swayed and rattled and Emily closed her eyes trying to remember what the street lamps were like when you were looking down on them from the top of the tram. At night you had a feeling of flying with shops and houses and people far below under the wavering lamplight. It was best of all when the streets were wet with rain and the lights were doubled, glimmering back up at you from the pavements. The swaying movement of the tram reminded her suddenly of the Slumberland Express and she never knew whether her father actually met them at the tram stop or whether she dreamed he did.

The Torch

SARAH sat over the remains of her lunch in the Luxembourg and carefully examined her freedom. For a few days after a journey, she had this disturbing sense of isolation both from home and from the place to which she had (however ardently) wished to escape. There were aspects of this stay in Paris that didn't bear too close scrutiny but she had no intention of disturbing the sunshine with them at the moment. She dismissed them. Ritually she wandered instead around her home as she tended to do at the start of any holiday seeing herself not there, seeing her empty room full of the debris she ought to have cleared away.

For a while she even accompanied her mother back into the silent house and observed the mechanical movements, sighing, tidying, glancing at the clock and wondering where Sarah was by now, if this time something might go wrong with a routine journey and if she would hear the phone ring telling of disaster. In one way at least she and her mother were alike. Ever since boarding school she had stood in the doorway of her room on the very point of departure. Maybe I shall never sleep in this room again. Never never again. Goodbye.

Sarah didn't think of her father in this interlocked way but as a sort of equal, free as she was herself to come and go and find meals to be late for in the appointed place. Smiling, she took from her canvas satchel a postcard of golden Madame Recamier and with fingers buttery on the biro she wrote:

Dear Denis, do I wish you were here? No! There isn't anywhere in the world I would rather be alone. Thanks for the money. The surveying job turned out to be for a firm which schemes to knock down all the parts of Paris I cherish, but for the moment I don't care, which must be immoral. It's lunchtime now and the sun is hot on my stretched out legs and my face is cool in the shade of a lime tree in the Luxembourg. The flat loaned to us by Kelly's aunt turns out to be an attic with red walls and white furniture and the view over the rooftops is pure corn. You can crane your neck and look under three bridges of the Seine, for God's sake, and who could ask for more? Kelly won't be here until the end of the month. Tomorrow I will write and tell mother so you needn't mention. . . .

She stopped writing and threw back a yellow ball to a child. Happiness at having been loaned a flat in the middle of Paris rendered her speechless for the moment. She remembered the Vendrons and their belief that a young visitor of fourteen should be satisfied with regular visits to the supermarket in the company of Madame and one accompanied hour a week at the Louvre. Still, they had taught her French and made this freedom possible now. She rolled over on the grass watching with half-closed eyes the coloured crowds go by. In one hour she had to meet O Lonargáin and it was an encounter she did not relish.

Deliberately dismissing his neglected teeth and his bristly red hair, she thought suddenly of her parents as two strangers whom she rather liked but found difficult in combination as indeed they probably found one another at this stage. Her mother six years ago had been different, given to sudden bursts of affection and laughter and always repentant over the notes she left in the kitchen when she would not be there during the holidays. Sarah at fourteen had not at first examined the possible reason. But once she had found her mother in tears after a phone call and it was as surprising as if she had found her father without trousers. For a while she had angrily resented it.

Denis had been the donor of lavish unexpected gifts – a tape-recorder, a typewriter, a sewing machine – given with the casualness of a bar of chocolate long ago. Her mother never gave large presents but she had never minded how many friends were gathered in for meals, had rather encouraged her to fill up the house. She even welcomed Peadar O Lonargáin whom she didn't really like.

Sarah knew she would be able to write to her mother once Peadar was out of the way. Tomorrow perhaps. In half an hour she had to meet the fellow which was a good reason for enjoying the time which was left until then. She took a walk along by the pond, twice bending to splash water on her hot face. Children sailing toy boats made her squat down with her sketch book to get the fluent movement of water and faces and circling hands, and by the time she had crumpled up the sketch in disgust it was time to go. On the way she uncrumpled the ball of paper from her pocket and leaned on her canvas satchel to add a few lines which she regarded as an improvement. Then she put the re-crumpled ball in a wastebasket and walked on through the lunchtime crowds to the metro entrance where Peadar O Lonargáin was waiting, leaning as always to one side like an old man. An accident with a gun had damaged one shoulder when he was a child in the country and it had been inexpertly treated by the local GP. Not that he would have been good-looking in any case. She remembered at Irish college long ago how she had forced herself to speak to him because he looked so lonely and ill at ease among the denim-clad city people like herself. His clothes were a decade out of date and he wore winter shoes which cut his heels. On Sarah's suggestion they had both gone barefoot to the beach every day. It had become a joke among the others.

She greeted him now in Irish and noticed how he still looked ill at ease and out of place in clothes more fit for a beach than for a street in Paris. The open-necked striped shirt was two sizes too big for him and his neck looked sore from the sun. He wore shapeless canvas trousers like an elderly American's, over which the shirt hung down pyjama-style. But on his feet were bright red espadrilles which looked as if the price tag might still be on them. When he smiled, the chipped front tooth she remembered from his childhood had grown darker than the rest as though dead at the roots. His voice was soft as ever and his Irish more richly perfect.

At the pavement café they drew glances because of the strange language and this made Sarah proud, as it made her illogically proud also when she was occasionally mistaken for a French girl in France.

'What you're asking me to do is distasteful in the extreme and you must know it. I've never made any effort to conceal the fact that I regard your activities and those of the rest as loathsome and criminal.'

'Would you have regarded your grandfather's fight for freedom as loathsome and criminal too, would you, Sarah?'

'That generation offered their *own* lives, not those of innocent civilians. There's no point of similarity in what your lot are doing and their insurrection.'

'Except love of Ireland,' he said passionately. 'Except willingness to offer our own lives as Burke and Neligan did in a stinking English jail last year. As Mannion may do any day now.'

'Burke and Neligan were murderous criminals who didn't mind maiming men, women and children in the London street bombings. If they were crooked enough to make themselves into martyrs by starving to death, it's irrelevant, completely unimportant. Whether Mannion lives or dies is of no importance to anyone but himself.'

'You were one of us once.' The voice was softer than ever now. She suddenly remembered the way he sang the last despairing cadences of 'An Droighnean Donn' long ago when they were young and the summer was just beginning.

'I was a schoolgirl then,' she said contemptuously, 'I

hadn't made up my mind about anything and I was still a victim of the cosy myths we all grew up on. Only I grew out of them. You and your lot never did. Returning the fourth green field to Mother Ireland is no good if there's nobody left to live on it, only carrion to suck up the blood. I'm going back to work. If you like I'll buy you dinner tonight for old time's sake, but only on condition you don't say a word about any of this again. OK?'

'You don't understand, Sarah.' The smile was gentler than ever now and the voice softer. He blinked the sore-looking eyes nervously, and unexpectedly covered her fingers with his hairy freckled hand. 'I wouldn't touch a hair of your head, Sarah, you know that. Whatever you did or didn't do. We've known one another too long and I'm too fond of you.'

'I think you've gone mad, Peadar.' Laughing incredulously, she tried to shake his hand away but he continued to pin hers to the table, the gentle distressed look never leaving his face. 'What *are* you talking about?'

'You wouldn't be too involved, and I'll tell them how you feel,' he urged. 'I'll tell them they can't count on you for anything else.'

'You'll tell them they can't count on me for this – how dare you convey veiled threats to me!' This time she got her hand free and felt like striking him with it. She took a sip of tepid beer instead and watched him crumple just the same as if she had struck him.

'You don't understand, Sarah,' he said again, 'O'Riain is here in Paris at the moment himself.'

'I hope he ends up behind bars again, where he belongs,' Sarah said. 'The dead guard at Portlaoise left seven children behind him, but he also left plenty of colleagues alive to take care of O'Riain.'

'He told me to tell you it's essential that the woman to handle this contact must have perfect French, so as to be indistinguishable from a French girl. It's half an hour's work, no more, Sarah. It involves you in nothing violent and if you do it I'll see you won't be asked again.'

'Goodbye, Peadar. I'm due back at work.'

'Listen, Sarah. . . .'

'Goodbye.'

'I'll try to find somebody else. . . .'

There was no anger in his face as she walked away, only the same look of distress and even shock. His face was so pale that the blotched freckles stood out like old scars, and she deliberately banished the memory of him as soon as she went up by lift to the office. Before the end of the afternoon a colleague came across through the rubber plants to tell her another Irish hunger-striker had died in London – the news had just come through on the transistor.

'Ah, bon,' Sarah said indifferently, and the French boy looked shocked as he returned to his place. It was the same boy who came running to tell her she was wanted on the telephone just as she was about to leave the office at four o'clock.

She couldn't believe it when she lifted up the phone and listened to the soft familiar rush of the Irish again. Her first impulse was to ring off, but it was a discourtesy she found beyond her. The voice of Peadar sounded older on the line, more gentle and more distressed even than when she had sat beside him this afternoon. He evaded the question of how he came to know where she worked and begged her to see him about a different matter for only a few minutes on her way home. He'd see her at the office entrance. Please.

'Very well.' It seemed the simplest way to hang up.

He had added an outsize Aran gansey to his strange assortment of clothes, and true to his word the whole matter didn't take too long. He had tried to contact two other possibilities in the course of the afternoon, but both had left Paris. He hadn't come back to ask her again. He accepted her refusal as final, but O'Riain did not. He had come to tell her not to return to the flat tonight. If she had friends, go to them, the further away the better. She must not, under any circumstances, go back to work tomorrow and she had better not return to Dublin either. When she laughed in his face he went even whiter and implored her to believe she was in danger. Then quite suddenly and faster than she had ever seen him move before, he vanished among the home-going crowds.

She stood for a few minutes irresolute on the pavement and in the late afternoon heat she felt cold. She thought of the Vendrons and the welcome she would certainly get if she went like last year with them to Avignon, but it wasn't possible. It was only above a certain level of self-respect that one could operate at all, and she knew that running away from her job was not something she could do even if she believed in this bad-movie sequence for which somebody had written her a part. Drawing a deep breath of comforting diesel fumes she moved quickly in the direction of the metro. Near Sacré Coeur she could buy bread and wine for supper.

Special Category

WHEN his number was called for a visit he couldn't quite believe it. His was not a travelling family although they were all involved one way or another with the railway. When the sergeant came rattling the keys he was not on his feet as presumably most of the other lucky prisoners were but still sitting on the edge of his bed, hands dangling between his knees, wondering who could possibly have managed to cross over and see him. Money was scarce at home and they might come to bury him but not otherwise.

'Get a move on there, Foxy,' the sergeant said without rancour. 'Or maybe you'd care to comb out the foxy head before the barber blows in one of these days. You won't have the hair long then, my lad, and we'll have to think up another name for ye, won't we? Name such as Skinny or summat.' His wheezy laugh was obviously well meant. This small red-nosed man was not the worst, not malicious like the tall good-looking sergeant who always singled him out for special baiting. The heavy coppery hair which had given B323 his family nickname seemed to annoy authority wherever he went, even before all this. It was difficult perhaps to look dutiful and dependable with a head of hair that flickered as though a searchlight were perpetually playing on it, that sprang into an imperial helmet of curls at the first touch of rain.

Now however in the yard where the prisoners exercised the sun beat down, stinging his eyes after the gloom of his cell. The sky was the same blue that had hardly darkened at all even when stars shone over the barricades during the fight. But that must be months ago now. He felt a little sleepy in the fresh air, unwilling to make the effort to look along the line of faces on the other side of the rough fencing to find his visitor. Finally B323 made an effort and ran his eye swiftly over the assembled faces, embarrassed or happy or shining with tears, none of them remotely familiar faces. His was not a visiting family, he reminded himself once again. He made an appeal to the red-nosed sergeant.

'Take me back, please, there's been some mistake. I know nobody here.'

'Sir,' the sergeant said.

'I know nobody here, sir.'

'Daft little foxy bastard,' the sergeant said amiably, although he was more than a foot shorter than the prisoner. 'There's been no bleeding mistake. Show ye.'

He left the line of military with fixed bayonets and went along the row of visitors, checking permits. B323 saw him stop and joke with a pretty girl in a straw boater with summery ribbons dangling between blue cotton shoulders. The gay dog made her laugh and shake her long hair, and then he returned to the only prisoner who hadn't found his visitor.

'Git over there, Foxy,' the sergeant said. 'Don't ye know your luck when ye see it? Nice little bit o' fluff she is too. Go over there and try her.' Baffled, the tall fiery prisoner walked over to the line of visitors and saw that the girl's eyes were speckled blue as a bird's egg and she was laughing again.

'Hello, Bartholomew Mullens. You're not a bit like I thought you'd be.'

'I'm sorry, but neither are you. My brother Paddy looks quite different.'

He had forgotten the sound of a girl's laugh, so he tried to make her laugh again. It was easy.

'I thought Bartholomew Mullens had to be small and spotty with a large Adam's apple and a very nice nature,' she said. 'I thought Bartholomew Mullens would have no way with the ladies and that I'd have to talk to him about his interests – butterfly catching, maybe, or stamp collecting, or the lives of the saints, or how nice it used to be down on his auntie's farm before he heard of Mother Ireland.'

'I never had an auntie with a farm, I'm sorry to say, and nobody ever calls me anything except – except Red Mull.'

She laughed so loudly at this that her elderly neighbour in black touched the girl's arm in reproof and put a finger to her lips. 'Sorry.' The girl giggled quietly then, before looking up at him under her summery hat. 'I'm Frances Montgomery from Dublin. And I *have* an auntie with a farm – here in Cheshire – who asked me over for a holiday.'

'But you haven't told me how you came to know my name?'

'I read the list of prisoners in the *Irish Times* book just before I came over. And I thought, poor Bartholomew Mullens, a boy with a name like that needs to be cheered up. When I saw you were in Knutsford I knew it was near where I was going so I wrote to the Governor and said I was your cousin and asked permission to visit you.'

'You're not a member of Cumann na mBan then?'

'Oh no, nothing like that. My mother would ask for her smelling salts at the mention of them. But my father's a bit of a rebel, always was. He gave me Mitchel's *Jail Journal* to read when I was ten and I've never been able to forget it. Have you ever read it?'

'If I hadn't I don't think I'd be here,' the prisoner said unguardedly, and to his consternation her eyes filled with tears, which she quickly blinked away. 'Also of course I saw William Butler Yeats's play *Cathleen Ní Houlihan*.'

'I saw it too in the Abbey Theatre,' the girl said eagerly, 'and when Michael went out after the Poor Old Woman I wanted to go with him. But next day I didn't. I wrote a poem about it instead.'

'Would you show it to me?'

'I might if you showed me some of yours.'

'How do you know I've written any?'

'Everyone of our age in Dublin writes poetry. Father says that's what's wrong with the country these days. Did anything you wrote get printed?'

He felt himself go red as his hair, and she pounced on this admission. Where was it printed, could she get copies?

'It was nothing,' he said at last. 'A few parodies and things like that. They were published in a little soft-covered book that sold for sixpence. Some of them also were printed in broadsheets. I set the verses to popular airs you could march to. They were supposed to be funny.'

'Could I get the book when I go back home? Could I buy it in Eason's?'

'Maybe. The publisher was the Art Depot in Mary Street – if Eason's haven't got it, the publishers might have a few copies left.'

'A poet,' she said, flatteringly awed. 'A poet who's been printed.'

'Now will you show me your poems?'

'I'll write to you when I get back home if I may, and I'll copy some out. The best one, any way. Will they let you have letters?'

'I don't know, he said. 'I haven't had any yet. I'll try to find out.'

'Father said it was "a poet's rebellion",' the girl remembered suddenly. 'Professor McDonagh and Patrick Pearse and Joseph Mary Plunkett. And now Bartholomew Mullins.'

'Do you know where they are now?' he said, smiling at his name tagged on among his betters. 'I never really found out for certain because we are not allowed newspapers and I've been in solitary for so long.'

'You mean you don't know?'

'The last time they asked me to sign the paper, they said people who wouldn't sign would be shot, but I didn't believe them.'

'This must be the promise to be of good conduct in future, and not to impede the war effort and so on?'

So this much was known outside? 'Yes.' He became aware for the first time of the other visitors around them, perhaps because the girl looked uneasy, as though she would like to go. The bell clanged out through the hot summer afternoon.

'I must go or maybe they won't let me come again,' she said, dipping her hand suddenly into the carpet-bag at her feet.

'Goodbye, Miss Montgomery, you are very good to come.'

'Please call me Fanny. I don't expect these cigarettes are the right brand or anything but maybe you could swap them. The rest of the stuff might be useful if you get hungry between meals. Jacob's biscuits from home.'

To his astonishment she smiled coaxingly as she put a big brown paper bag into his hands and was gone before he could thank her. But she hadn't answered his question and even as he called her she was running back.

'They shot Patrick Pearse with two others on the third of May. I remember because it was my birthday.'

'And the rest of the leaders?'

'They shot all the signatories of the Proclamation – on different days at the end of April and early May.'

'Connolly too? We heard at the barricades he was badly hurt.'

'Connolly too,' she said. 'I'll come to see you again, Red Mull, if they let me.'

'God go with you, Fanny. Don't forget the poem, will you?'

'I won't forget but it's not good. Remember it was I who said it.' And she was gone. The last he saw of her was the back of the straw hat with its tossing ribbons among the dark clothes of the other women.

Almost at once the red-nosed sergeant was at his side. 'Told ye she was a nice little bit o' fluff, Foxy, didden I?' he whispered. 'Open up the dibs, there, till we see wot she brought yer. Blimey, bloody millionaires she must come from. Player's Navy Cut – a whole bloody box o' smokes –

Fry's creamy chocolate and Jacob's biscuits. Some blokes 'as all the luck, Foxy me lad.'

'If you come to my cell tonight you can have your share of all this, sergeant. I suppose the bag has to be inspected now for hand grenades or something?'

'Ye never knows yer luck – might be allowed keep the lot, Foxy. But I doubt it.'

'Meaning what?'

'Meaning tuck and that is for chappies as signs their paper, see? You said no, Foxy, four times by all I hear.'

'That's right, sergeant. And I'll continue to say no.'

'Well, same as I said, ye never knows yer luck. Quick march now, look sharp.'

At the entrance to the prisoner's own block, the bag was taken away from him and he was told he might have some of the contents returned to him later. The block officer scribbled the prisoner's number on the outside of the bag. B323, followed by a question mark.

'I request permission, sir, to smoke one of those cigarettes now.' Even as he heard himself speaking, he despised himself.

'Permission refused.'

'I request permission then for pencil and paper.'

'Permission also refused. Return the prisoner to his quarters, sergeant.'

'Yes, sir.'

Before the cell door clanged behind him the sergeant whispered. 'Do wot I can for ye later, Foxy.'

Dead, all dead.

Connolly and Pearse and McDonagh and McBride and Plunkett and Clarke and Eamon Ceannt. All dead, while he bent the knee to the extent of asking for a lousy cigarette. He sat on the edge of his plank bed and watched his hands shaking.

For a few days death was far away from the adventure of Cuckoo Lane. Death was distant gunfire magnified by the golden air and the full river opposite the Four Courts. A

shell which had burst in O'Connell Street (they were told)
bounced in successive waves of sound under the four bridges
and then seemed to explode in diamonds against the river
wall. But nobody suffered more than sore eardrums. The
dead were somewhere else. The small company of men left
briefly in his charge by Commandant Daly had laughed like
schoolboys (which two of them were) when he sang his own
parody for them – 'Come Along and Join the British Army'.
They were tired and dirty but not sleepy, although most of
them had had no sleep for four nights. The girls billetted
in the nearby Father Matthew Hall had looked after them
well, and being a soldier was something new and interesting
after the routine of normal life. Sometimes on the night
watch he was back in brief waves of weariness on the footplate of his engine, watching the golden showers of sparks
that flew like a shaken flag in the night sky when he opened
the refuelling hatch on the long dark trip to Galway.
Shovelling coal, his face black, he often laughed then to
think of his other very private life, the elocution lessons he
paid for out of what his mother left him from his wages, the
Irish lessons at the Conradh office in Parnell Square, the
dizzy day he was auditioned for the Abbey Theatre when
the poet said. 'Interesting what you have managed to do
with the voice of a callow young student from Trinity, Mr
Fay,' and Mr Fay replied, pleased. 'This is not the student,
Mr Yeats. This is a young fireman from the Midland and
Great Western Railway – he never went beyond the seventh
book, but as you see he met the scholars coming home. He
writes songs too.'

They exchanged a little laugh. 'He might do for Michael,
don't you think, if the other boy can't attend rehearsals,'
Mr Yeats said, 'and this remarkable red hair would look
well on stage.' 'I was hoping you'd say that. The red hair
would indeed be right,' Mr Fay replied. They spoke as if
he weren't there but he didn't mind that. In the end he did
play Michael for a whole week, and maybe it was that which
decided him about joining the Volunteers. The frightening

silence of the theatre, the wave of emotion that broke over
the packed bodies he couldn't see, excited him like wine as
he waited for his cue from Miss Allgood's breathtaking lines
every night.

Many that are red-cheeked now will be pale-cheeked;
many that have been free to walk the hills and the bogs
and the rushes will be sent to walk hard streets in far
countries; many a good plan will be broken; many that
have gathered money will not stay to spend it; many a
child will be born and there will be no father at its
christening to give it a name. They that have red cheeks
will have pale cheeks for my sake, and for all that they
will think they are well paid.
            They shall be remembered for ever.
            They shall be alive for ever. . . .

Somewhere between the theatre and the red footplate in
the darkness the desire to follow Tone and Mitchel and fight
for his country was born and he knew why he was never for
a moment affected by the recruiting posters all over the city:
'Your Country Needs YOU.' His country perhaps did
need him, but his country wasn't England. It was a shadowy
place the speeches of Patrick Pearse and the journal of John
Mitchel and the heady lines of William Butler Yeats had
suddenly brought very close. It was Inis Ealga or Banba or
Fodhla, and its queen had big eyes that blazed like Maud
Gonne's. There were some that called her the Poor Old
Woman and there were some who called her Cathleen the
daughter of Houlihan.

At the barricades in Cuckoo Lane he knew his job in the
railway was gone for ever and that his family might even
disown a member so foolish as to disemploy himself in these
hard times, but he didn't care. He didn't see any further
than the starry April sky that was soft like summer and the
comradeship that was like nothing he had ever known before.
A thin girl of whom Fanny Montgomery reminded him

used to come with food for them from the Father Matthew Hall. He was always worried that a stray bullet might kill or injure her on her way over to Cuckoo Lane and one night he told her so, offering to ask Commandant Daly if he might convey her back. She laughed at him. 'Every time I get safely over and back to the Hall I get a great big thrill out of it,' she said, and he knew then that she reacted as he did to the great adventure.

When it was over he couldn't believe that only six days had passed since the night he packed his kit bag in the kitchen at home after his family had gone to bed. In the farewell note to his mother he had said, 'Don't worry about me – this is why I was born and I've never been more content. God keep you all till I see you again when we've taught John Bull a lesson and set old Ireland free. In case of a raid, burn this letter from your loving son, Red Mull.'

She wasn't like the schoolboy's mother who had come to the barricades and shamed him in front of the men, begging him to come home before he got killed. She wasn't like the student's mother who had brought him a change of clothes and passed it through the railings of the Rotunda Gardens where they had lain all night after surrender. She wasn't like the rossies who had sniggered under their shawls when the band of dirty beaten men who were his comrades staggered out next morning into the sunshine of shattered O'Connell Street opposite Crane's Musical Emporium.

'A fine pack of chocolate soldiers youse are to be freeing oul' Ireland – Jasus, would you look at the cut of the Irish Volunteers!' a brassy young one had called out, and for the first time he and his companions had looked at one another. Tired eyes, dusty clothes, week-old beards, stiff and aching limbs through which they tried to get the blood moving again. A fine pack of chocolate soldiers indeed, but spurred by their own dismal appearance they had marched smartly enough to the Richmond Barracks. In the gymnasium they were told to lie down on the floor and then the identification by Dublin G-men began. One by one, as the long hot day wore on, the important prisoners were weeded out: Joe McGuinness, Eamon Duggan, Ned Daly, J. J. Walsh, Dinny O'Callaghan and the old Fenian signatory, Tom Clarke.

Neither to these men nor to anybody else was food or drink offered, and beside him Mullens remembered the sick moaning of the schoolboy who had refused to go home with his mother. 'If only I had a sup of water, Mullens,' the boy kept whimpering over and over again and at last he could stand it no longer but wriggled unseen as a snake past man after man until he reached an open window. It was dusky now, but still warm, and underneath a sentry passed and repassed with clicking heels along the yard. Under cover of a few men who saw what he was doing, Mullens leaned over the window sill. 'Could you get me a cup of water, please, Tommy, for a sick man,' he said softly, and the sentry just as softly cursed the seed and breed of all bloody Fenian Paddies. In the end he agreed to a bucketful for two shillings, with a cup thrown in, and Mullens's only fear was that the water would never last as far as the schoolboy. Men whose lips were sore and cracked with thirst clawed at the bucket as it passed. A change of guard made it possible for other deals to be made however with the Tommies in the yard and soon the thirst at least of everybody was quenched. It was to be hours later before the oblong hard dog biscuits were offered to them and by then their fate had been sealed.

> Come along and join the British Army
> Show that you're not afraid
> Put your name upon the roll of honour
> In the Dublin Pals' Brigade.
> We'll send you out to die in France or Belgium
> 'Twill prove that you are true blue,
> When the war is over if we want you any more
> We'll find you in the SDU.

The men had urged him to sing for them as they rocked jam-packed to transportation in the old Slieve Bloom. A soldier had tried to batten down the hatches before she set sail but Mullens had spoken up. 'If you want us to survive to be properly chastised, Tommy, that's not the way.' The men roared in approval, and later an officer checked the situation and ordered the hatches to be left open.

'Give us a few bars there, Mullser, one of your own,' somebody shouted as they pulled out into Dublin Bay, so he led them in singing one of his parodies. Once a song of his had been sung in the Queen's Music Hall and he had been delighted but never thought he might be paid money for such things: he had no idea how the little published collection was faring. He could write better ones now if he could only get his hands on paper and pencil, but that had been refused for months now. He thought of paper with the same greed as he thought of food when he was hungry (which was almost always). He thought of fat lined copy-books and scribbling pads and pads of coloured notepaper and the comforting fat feel of a pencil between his fingers, his favourite kind of pencil which couldn't be rubbed out, a copying ink pencil that turned purple when you spat on it. But any pencil would do, or any broken-down N pen, any half-dried powdery ink. If they'd allow him writing materials he could endure the lack of books and newspapers. Without either and totally without news of home, he sometimes felt like beating his head off the wall.

Since it was clear from what the girl had said that lists of some kind had been published, why hadn't any of his family written to him? They had been against all this of course, thought it criminally neglectful of a son to risk the loss of his job or the loss to them of thirty shillings out of his two pound wage packet, but he didn't think they would go so far as not to write to him. Not his mother anyway. When he went on his holidays – for which he wasn't paid and had to save – she was content with only a pound a week from him to be paid her before going away. Plenty of parents, he knew demanded the usual lot, holidays or no holidays.

A key sounded suddenly in the lock, and he knew from

the thickened blue light behind his barred window that it must be supper-time. It wasn't, however. The good-looking, swarthy sergeant had come to pay a visit, a sheet of paper in his hand. The prisoner got reluctantly to his feet.

'Good evening, sir,' the sergeant prompted.

'Good evening.'

The prisoner shrugged as though at a tiresome child and mimicked the exact tone. The blow across the mouth was only moderately painful, being expected.

'I can loan you a pen, B323, which is a lot more than you deserve.'

'I'm much obliged to you, sir. If you could prolong the loan and manage a little paper as well I'd regard it as a great favour. I've been asking for both since I came here, sir.'

'The only paper you need is in my hand. If you don't sign, I'm instructed to leave you without supper – and by the same token, without any benefit from your food parcel – tonight. If you do sign, there's 'am and heggs waiting in the galley. You can be off tomorrow at dawn with a one-way ticket home in your pocket. Sign here, please.'

The sergeant bent his handsome oiled black head and drew out the triangular table which was bracketted to the wall. 'Sit down, B323. Make yourself at home.'

'No thank you, sir. I've already stated my reasons for not wishing to sign.'

'Read the bleedin' paper again, you stubborn Irish bastard, and see that it's a reasonable exchange for your freedom.'

'I'll recite the most offensive passage by heart for you, sergeant, if you like.' It wasn't for nothing he'd sweated learning lines between stoking sessions on the footplate. 'Being liable to continued detention in internment under the Defence of the Realm Act for the duration of the war, I hereby undertake if released from internment not to engage in any act of a seditious nature or any act calculated to hinder the successful prosecution of the war. Whose war, sergeant? It's not our war, the Germans were the friends of Ireland. Besides, who is to decide what an act of a "seditious character" is? Might not playing in one of Mr Yeats's plays be judged to be one? Signing a paper like this would be signing myself into bondage, not freedom.'

'Mere formality,' the sergeant said lightly. 'That's what your mates think all over the lock-up. Seven more went 'ome today.'

'Believe me, I appreciate your concern on my behalf, sir. But there's no change in my attitude.'

'There may be a change in ours though, Paddy, see if there mayn't.' The threat was accompanied by a final wave of the document in front of his face and the banged iron door left echoes that bounced several times from wall to wall. When the footsteps died away along the cage walk the prisoner decided he had earned the treat he didn't often allow himself. He bent and picked with his fingers at the flaking whitewash under the place where the table was set into the wall. When you chewed the limey stuff, hunger was baffled after a while and you almost forgot you hadn't eaten. You could spit away what remained in your mouth into the brown porcelain charlie in the corner and pray it would be dissolved in piss before anybody noticed. There was some water in the metal jug still, and he drank that after he'd finished chewing. Tepid dusty stuff it was but it served. There would be nothing better on offer tonight.

He lay down on the bedboards and watched the thickening of the summer light through the bars. If he'd been fed he knew he could have passed the time more pleasurably with forbidden fantasies of girls he knew at home, but now he could think of them only as remote beauties like Mary Pickford or Clara Bow. Somewhere a church bell sounded and somewhere else a dog barked, shrill and prolonged. Barking perhaps for his supper? He would eat slightly fatty scraps of good meat from the family table and maybe some leftover gravy and potatoes. He would maybe finish off with a hard delicious heel of crusty bread and wash it all down with a bowl of cool fresh water. Lucky dog. Finding a good angle for his shoulder-blades, the prisoner let his mind

stray lecherously over visions of food, big plates of fragrant
smoked bacon and egg with Hafner's sausages, creamy
dishes of tripe and onions, Sunday roasts of rich beef with
juice running down the crispy sides to be soaked up in the
pan by roasting potatoes, rabbit stew savoury with sage and
snowy dumplings, tender pink slices of boiled bacon with
green cabbage curling in its juices, and in the centre of the
scrubbed table at home a mountain of floury potatoes for the
taking, bought in sacks by his driver father in some place
like Mullingar or Ballinasloe. Afterwards maybe a spicy
apple cake with a frosted sugar garnish or newly baked
raisin bread with the golden topping his sister gave it by
smearing the round loaves with beaten egg before arranging
them in the oven. Then he thought of Frances Montgomery
with her summery straw hat and her Jacob's biscuits (what
kind? ginger snaps or butter creams or fig rolls, puff
cracknels or all sorts of sugar biscuits with brightly coloured
tops?) Who would eat her Fry's cream chocolate, from
whose lucky mouth would cloud the smoke from her
Player's cigarettes?

If he'd had the wit to ask her, she might smuggle him
paper and pencil some time and he might get away with it
hidden next his skin. But more than likely she'd go home
and he'd never see her again. She had told him her father
was a journalist on the staff of the *Freeman's Journal* and she
lived in a house on the Drumcondra Road near the Bishop's
Palace. It wasn't likely he'd ever see her again but he'd
never forget her either, herself and her summery hat and
her laugh and her Jacob's biscuits. He was almost asleep,
almost happy, when the iron key turned in the iron door and
he was rasped awake again.

'No more bye-byes, Foxy, got a bitta comfort for ye here.'
The sergeant smelled comfortably of his evening beer and
his unlovely face was benevolent. His offerings were a
crumpled cigarette and a hard army biscuit which he took
squashed together from his pocket. Beside them in the
prisoner's outstretched hand he placed two melting squares

of dark Bourneville chocolate half in, half out of their silver wrapping. Better still, he splashed fresh water into the metal jug.

'Not a beanfeast maybe, Foxy, but the best I could muster from stock,' he apologised, and the prisoner made long appreciative noises before he spoke his thanks.

'Home was never like this, sergeant.'

'Betcher sweet life it weren't,' the sergeant said. 'Not that you'll see homeland for many a long day yet. Wot's in a bitta paper they want signing, tell me that?'

'I'll save the chocolate and the fag for later,' the prisoner sidetracked. 'I'm much obliged to you for your kindness, sergeant. I hope I'll be able to do something for you some day.'

'Not if you don't sign their blasted paper, you won't. Two more of your blokes gone this morning.'

'Gone home, you mean?'

'Gone to hell, the boss says, for not signing. Shot, mate.' By this time the sergeant was sitting companionably on the boards beside him. 'What's in it, Foxy . . . tell me that.'

The prisoner was by now luxuriously biting noisy morsels off the hard biscuit which smelled of tobacco, and shaking his flaming head at the same time.

'I wish I could make you understand, sergeant. What I took part in wasn't just a brawl or a week-long riot as we heard some of your newspapers made out. It was a national movement, a revolution, to assert once again in arms the right of the Irish people to independence after seven hundred years of foreign misrule – yours, that is. Our leaders were professors and poets and idealists, men who knew we hadn't a chance militarily, although we didn't do too badly in the scrap to tell the truth of us. Now they are all dead, shot in revenge by your government which wants us to fight your war for you when we have no freedom ourselves. I'll make no apology and no promises to be of better behaviour in future just to be free to walk out of here when better men than me were glad and proud to give up their lives. "Wrap the Green Flag Round Me, Boys,'' was what we sang when Commandant Pearse ordered us to surrender to save innocent lives, and we marched through the ruins of O'Connell Street on the first lap to the transportation ships. Listen sergeant, listen and I'll tell you what we sang.' His big young voice filled the cell:

> 'And though my body moulders, boys,
> My spirit will be free,
> And every comrade's honour, boys will
>   still be dear to me,
> And in the thick and bloody fight
> Nor let your courage lag
> For I'll be there and hovering near
> Around the dear old flag.'

'You've a nice bleeding voice,' the sergeant said. But it's all a load of bullshit and codswallop. You're too bloody young to know, Foxy, that no country is worth dying for, and all dear old flags are the same if they're wrapped around your stinking corpse. Sign their bleeding paper and get out of here and live for your country like the rest of them.'

'Living dishonourably ever after is not my cup of tea. I'd rather moulder as the song says.'

'Honour – dishonour!' The sergeant's red face glowed more fiercely. 'Words the quality thinks up over their mulled port wine and their big fat cigars. I was with those men lying for weeks in stinking trenches in Flanders until their feet rotted off them in one night's frost. I went off my rocker for a while meself after a shell burst beside me and I'm glad to say they invalided me out and set me watching blokes as refused to fight – bloody right they are too. Don't talk to me about honour and dishonour and the glory of bloody war. A fat lot of honour your poor bastard the general had when they set him up like an Aunt Sally at a fair. They tied him to a chair because his rotting foot wouldn't hold him up long enough to be shot dead. There's glory for ye!'

'That was General Connolly, I suppose?'

'Never could remember Paddies' names,' the sergeant said. 'Sweet dreams, Foxy.'

'Could you get me a stub of pencil and some paper, sergeant? Anytime?'

'Maybe tomorrow, Foxy. Get to bye-byes now and pray Captain Allen don't do you for a troublesome bastard as he means to.'

'Meaning?'

'Goodnight, Foxy, me lad. No more questions tonight.'

The thought of the half-promised pen and paper, the fag and the precious chocolate, kept him going until the gas lamps bubbled their greenish light through the Judas hole. So long as he didn't smoke and didn't eat any more tonight, he had smoking and eating stored away for the taking. He drew the unlit cigarette luxuriously under his nostrils and he sniffed too at the homely smell of dark chocolate. On Saturdays his father would divide two bars of Bourneville among the six of them, and on Sundays his mother sometimes made them Fry's creamy cocoa instead of tea. She was harsh about money but she kept a good table, his mother.

Smelling that cocoa once again in his mind, he hid behind the door the crumpled cigarette and the square of chocolate. Then he had a long drink of fresh water and lay down on the planks once more, still smelling cocoa, determinedly putting the captain out of his mind. He couldn't pray, even, since the priests refused absolution to men going off with packed kit bags. He fell asleep at last with a steaming mug of cocoa warming his hands and the next minute the key rasped again in the door of his cell.

Only it wasn't the next minute, because a thin grey light showed through the bars of his window. Morning. And a soldier he had never seen before was standing with fixed bayonet ready to escort him somewhere. The soldier agreed to wait until the night's secretions had been deposited in the brown vessel in the corner and then he marched the prisoner before him along the silent cat cage. There was no sound yet from the other prisoners, no sound anywhere except their own echoing footsteps. They stopped before a small square room bright with several gaslights turned up full. Captain Allen looked spruce, combed and shaved except for his little moustache, and there was a smile in his handsome black eyes. He was sitting at a small table with pen, ink and paper before him.

'That will do, Parfitt. You may leave the prisoner until I call you.'

'Very good, sir.'

'You may wish me good morning, B323.'

'Good morning, Captain Allen.'

'Sir.'

'Sir.' The prisoner's shrug was hardly perceptible, but noted.

Captain Allen smiled, with the white well-brushed teeth. 'I have something here I'd like you to identify, B323, if you would be so kind. How it came into my possession needn't concern you. Read it, if you please.'

The prisoner was given into his astonished hands a broadsheet he knew very well. He had several copies of it at home. 'Songs of Freedom' was the heading and three of the parodies had come from his own hand. He had had the satisfaction of hearing one of them sung in a fine big baritone voice by the postman doing his first rounds in Broadstone when he himself had been hurrying home from the night mail to bed. It was to this parody the officer's pink finger with its white half-moon was pointing now.

'Read it if you please, B323.' The order was softly repeated and the prisoner took the broadsheet into his hand. The temptation was irresistible, and before he had consciously made a decision he heard his own voice ring out to the tune of 'Whack Fol the Diddle', managing to get through almost a complete stanza.

'Joe Devlin sure he cannot grouse
Whack fol the diddle lol the di-do-day
For now he's "Leader" of the House
Whack fol the diddle lol the di-do-day
The party men stand overawed
As Joe their slavery does applaud. . . .'

The prisoner saw the pistol-blow coming but he went on singing until the stars burst in his head and his mouth seemed to be full of blood. When a glass of water was shakily offered him he took it and rinsed away into the proferred ashtray a broken side tooth from the lower jaw. When he looked up again at the officer's face it was ugly with bitterness and shame for what he had done.

'A semi-literate peasantry has ruined the planned progress of two parliamentary generations. We had Home Rule in the palm of our hand as soon as the war is over, but that wouldn't do the Paddywhacks – the brutish unthinking urban and rural peasantry, that hasn't changed for two hundred years.'

'We?' the prisoner repeated, dabbing at his thickening lips with a handkerchief that had been given him, '*We*?'

'Do you think, my nearly-literate friend, that yours is the only sort of patriotic Irishman? Do you?'

The prisoner smiled and said once again that the leaders of this rebellion had been professors, poets, philosophers. He felt a sort of pity for the impassioned fellow Irishman with his handsome eyes and his pretty pink fingernails like a girl's. For a moment he thought conversation, even argument, might be possible. But the officer jabbed a handbell on his desk, and violently ordered the sergeant to take the prisoner away.

They were recalled from half the length of the corridor and the familiar paper for signing was proferred, even with some gentleness. The prisoner shook his flaming head and the order to return him to his cell was given once again. He was no sooner there than a sergeant he had not seen before appeared at the door and ordered him to remove his clothes and boots. Dressed only in his coarse regulation drawers, the prisoner was marched through many corridors of the awakening prison to a wing that seemed miles away and silent as the other was busy.

The footsteps of the unknown sergeant rang out and returned in a hollow echo. The prisoner's bare feet made no sound. He was already very cold, and his lower jaw ached persistently, like his head. A distant clock chimed seven times as they came to a large door at the end of a stone passage. This was unlocked with some difficulty, the prisoner was ushered into a comparatively large square room with windows high up in the wall, and the door banged heavily behind the retreating guard.

It was so cold in the room that it might have been January instead of July. There was no comfort in the foggy grey light filtering through the windows and none for bare feet on the clean stone floor. But there was one good thing about it all the same. The room was big enough to run around and this the prisoner did, briskly from corner to corner, until, presumably, the guard would get back with a change of clothes. More felonious garments still? A hair shirt, perhaps, or shoes with spikes inside?

Once the blood got moving through his body again, he felt almost cheerful and quite equal to enduring the throb in his jaw. He found with his tongue the place where the broken tooth had been and he tasted blood again. But if all he got out of joining a revolution was a broken tooth, he was lucky. Even his feet didn't feel so cold now, but he kept running around on his toes anyway until he was exhausted. Then he set the bedboards on the trestles and lay down, a little exhilarated even as he waited for the guard to come down again with clothes and maybe even breakfast.

There was, however, no sound nearer than a distant clop of horseshoes on cobbled streets and he lay back listening as intently as the blood drumming in his ears would allow. A faraway dog gave a volley of short sharp barks and was silent again. A church bell sounded, and then a shrill prolonged whistle as a train pulled into the faraway station. This was the homeliest sound of all and suddenly he was with the men on the footplate in the bustle of arrival, with them in the warm carriage-slamming world of another journey safely over, in the steaming splash of hot water and the rough comfort of the clean coarse towels, with them most of all as they sat gossipping over their steaming mugs of strong tea or sank their teeth into the crustiness of new bread. He closed his eyes and concentrated hard on hearing the first sounds that could mean his own approaching breakfast, but there were none, no familiar sound at all of an ordinary prison morning. Rather did the faint sounds that came to him now connect him with the unknown Cheshire town outside where ordinary people were beginning their day's work.

He thought he dozed for a while, but the cold woke him up again and he began again the pacing of his cell. His flesh was goosepimply now and his feet like ice again. He was evidently being punished for not signing the paper, or for cheekily singing 'Election Results' for the captain with the silky voice, but why had his clothes been taken away? As his hunger raged on he thought lustfully of the two squares of chocolate and the squashed fag hidden in his cell, and he hoped if he never went back to claim them some other poor starving bastard would have the wit to find them. This gave him an idea and he searched his spacious new quarters with care.

Nothing. Not a crumb on the table, or caught in the back of the chair. Not even a break in the smooth white plaster of the walls, so eventually he set to behind the door where it might escape notice. His fingers were cold and it was hard to make the first break but he struck at the wall with the chair at last and was rewarded with a few flakes of plaster that tasted quite as good as the stuff in his own cell. There was no water to wash them down but he supposed they couldn't leave him for ever without water. He started to run around his cell again until he realised that this made him thirstier so he stretched out on the bed again and lay with closed eyes willing his mind elsewhere, along the banks of the Royal Canal in March when swans nested among the greening weed, sitting for weeks on their ramshackle nests formed from rubbish people threw into the canal. As a child he used to watch for signs of the young ones, big grubby ungainly chicks that Hans Andersen wrote a story about. His thoughts idling among the reedy banks in sunshine, he was unprepared for the pistol shots, four of them that suddenly ripped into his consciousness.

He remembered the sergeant's words last night: 'Two more of your blokes gone today . . . to hell, the Captain says.' The thought that he might be shot, that the execution yard might be here, this side of the jail, made him sit up sharply, forgetting that with his damaged jaw he should move slowly. Pain throbbed into his neck and up into the crown of his head and he sat for what seemed a long time on the edge of the boards, waiting for more shots. There were none. He thought perhaps his own execution might be the next, and that it would be heard by some other naked poor devil in a cell somewhere in the honeycomb.

He reminded himself that from the moment he packed his kit bag on that night of disputed mobilisation, he had known it might be for the last time. But he had known and agreed that he might be signing on for his own death long before, from the moment the small recruiting handbill caught his eye in the window of Shanahan's in Cuffe Street. That was March last year, nesting time along the Canal.

EMMET DIED TO FREE IRELAND. WHAT ARE *You* DOING
TOWARDS THIS GLORIOUS OBJECT?
WHAT I CAN DO:
JOIN A VOLUNTEER COMPANY WHICH WILL TRAIN
YOU TO BEAR ARMS IN IRELAND'S CAUSE.

They had trained him to bear arms in Ireland's cause

every Friday night between eight and ten o'clock in St Joseph's Hall, and they had taught him to jump and vault properly which might be useful to an actor if he ever made the full-time grade, and they had taught him signalling and first-aid and musketry. He had been commended for his progress and he had shown up well on rainy weekend manoeuvres in the Dublin mountains. Only that he sometimes came to meetings in his fireman's uniform straight off the job, he thought he might have been made an officer, but it didn't worry him. He accepted that the officers always wore a collar and tie and had neatly kept hands that seldom lifted anything heavier than a pen. Born himself to hard manual work and the necessity to conduct his own education if he wanted that luxury, he admired their patiently acquired toughness in the field, the way they ignored blistered hands and feet and cold and exposure which to him were normal. He remembered most of all the bravery of Commandant Daly during the fight and the way his men always came first, first for food, first for rest.

He remembered the day he had come closest to his commanding officer after the week's fiercest battle when they found the six mown-down British Tommies in a heap together near the head of Church Street, like boys who had tumbled over in a game. He knew that Ned Daly and himself were united in not seeing them any more as the ancient enemy but as sons and brothers who would never go home any more and who hadn't even the glory of dying out on the Western Front. Their families and friends would see this as death in a brawl in Ireland, stupid, ignoble, soon to be forgotten like other brawls. Death by accident almost. A pity but not a glory, nothing to boast of as their death in Flanders would have been. Yet the fact of their death was the same. Their lives were over, and like himself they were not yet twenty. Flies were feasting on the open face of one of them, and Commandant Daly covered it with the boy's fallen cap.

The prisoner suddenly remembered that Ned Daly, like

Pearse and Connolly, must be dead now, who had been gentle with death. He made the sign of the cross and tried again to pray, but then he remembered hearing that some priests had even refused absolution to dying Volunteers. These cowardly men of God were worse than the Carthaginians in whose power he was now. Carthaginians Mitchel had called them (as he had called the Catholic church 'the enemy of Irish freedom') even although they allowed him books and the materials to write his Journal. Pen and ink actually to write the words that now came unbidden back to him – had he ever learned them, as he'd learned Michael's lines or did they stay imprinted on his mind for ever from the moment he read them?

'We must openly glorify arms until young Irishmen burn to handle them and try their temper; and this we must do in defiance of the "law" – deny that it is law; deny that there is any power in the London parliament to make laws for us and declare that as a just God ruleth in the earth we shall obey such laws no longer.'

He shouted the words out loud, jumped up from the planks and beat with his fist on the door and shouted them again. There were no Carthaginians around to hear but that couldn't be helped. At the top of his voice he shouted again what Mitchel had shouted to his Journal, that he would 'hurl the fires of Hell at the British Empire' before he signed a paper implicitly apologising for what he had done and promising to be of good behaviour in future. In future? What future?

His hands fallen by his sides, he realised for the first time the significance of the large, almost comfortable cell and the remote empty wing. This was where they sent men to be away from the rest of the prisoners at the end. This was the condemned cell and these were his last hours. It was all nonsense what he had heard about the fags and the good food you got before they shot you. He had been jailed without trial and now he would be dispatched without food and worst of all without the stub of a pencil to make his

farewells or write his testament. The fellow Irishman with
the beautiful hands had taken sophisticated revenge for the
gross impertinence of a prisoner's behaviour. If it be so,
Mitchel used to say, be it so. No crumpled letter of farewell
to his family or comrades, no scribbled word of thanks to
Frances Montgomery of some place near the Bishop's
Palace. All around her hat she might even wear a tri-
coloured ribbon O – if only she knew. If she came to see
him again what would they tell her? Would word be sent
to his mother? Shot while trying to escape? That was
sufficient excuse, he believed.

He looked up at the small high window and saw that it was
filling with honey light brimming through the bars. With
his back against the cold cell door he listened deliberately
to the morning and thought he could distinguish the rattle
of milk carts and again the distant clop of hooves on cobble-
stones. The town clock struck and he counted the strokes.
Seven. Seven o'clock of a July morning, maybe the last
morning of his life. If he were sure he could look it in the
face and not be afraid. 'For from the graves of patriot men
and women spring living nations,' Commandant Pearse had
said over the grave of the old Fenian. Pearse and all his
comrade leaders were lying in such graves now, all together
in quicklime maybe, for all he knew. It didn't perhaps
matter where one died, or how solitary the grave. What
mattered was not being afraid, and in humility making the
sacrifice of what poor future one believed one had. He didn't
think he was afraid. Starved and still cold he was, despite
the warm honey-coloured light, but not afraid. 'Be my prison
where it will, I suppose there is a heaven above that place,'
Mitchel had said, and he too supposed there was. But if he
had the choice between the slim books of the New Testament
and the thumb-tattered *Jail Journal* he kept beside his bed
at home, he knew which he would choose. He was what the
books he had read and the lines that had been a trumpet call
had made him and all he had to offer was his own life such
as it was. He'd like (who wouldn't?) to have fallen with his

leaders, to have gone out in a blaze during Commandant Daly's great fight. He would like (and the wish he knew was an arrogant wish) to have added his life physically to theirs though he wasn't a leader and had only followed in a lighthearted even frivolous way. And so his death would be like the deaths of the poor English bastards in North King Street, an afterthought, a sort of accident, not really related to the sum total of the sacrifice. But no matter. He knew he wasn't afraid and that was something. It could be that when the town clock struck eight he would be standing blindfold in the sunny yard, wearing some sort of clothes, he hoped, and not, positively not, afraid to die. He might be afraid of a hanging death, but he had heard the shots off and on during the summer that meant somewhere men had died. He supposed shooting was quicker and cheaper than hanging and that was why Irish prisoners were shot when necessary rather than as the concession to them of a soldier's death. No green flag after all would be wrapped around him, but to hell with that. The worst he had to put up with until eight o'clock was the itch to write, anything even his name. Bent on one knee he tried to scratch it behind the door with his fingernail but it wasn't very successful. If they brought him even a bowl of gruel he knew he could scratch something with his spoon, but they wouldn't feed him now. Breakfast was long over. And what need had a man of breakfast when his life had dwindled to one hour from now?

But one hour from then he was incredulously listening to the town clock striking eight, pleasant mellow notes in the summer air. There were no other sounds, no scrape of boots or clatter of bayonets as an armed guard came to conduct him into the yard. No sounds of any kind except the distant hum of the town that was no more than the purring of a giant cat unless one deliberately listened for and distinguished one small sound or another. He did that for a long time later on as he grew warmer with the day outside and so far beyond the edges of hunger that he didn't feel it any more. He could still offer no prayers but he spoke aloud

James Clarence Mangan, and Emmet's speech from the dock, and some of Tom Moore, and 'The Night Before Larry Was Stretched', and he tried to continue with a comic parody he was making to the air of 'The Harp and Lion'.

> 'Says Dan when I met him one day
> A word with you I'd like to say –
> Kate's hand in love you'll ne'er attain
> Except you give up this Sinn Féin
> Sore heads and cranks the "Freeman" calls you
> Even that does not. . . .'

Does not what? Does not appal you? Doesn't rhyme but it will do for the moment. His voice rang out and echoed and died away but he kept up the pastime. It wasn't a very good parody but then he'd noticed that it wasn't the very good ones people took up. Frequently the contrary. He had three more verses (knowing how much better they would be if only he had paper and a stub of pencil) when he noticed the light was fading and somehow the day had worn away.

He was pattering around the stone floor to ease his cramped limbs again when he heard the first sounds (for how many hours?) in this wing. A laugh and the scrape of boots and a bayonet jingle. He leaped at the door and battered on it with his fists, shouting at the top of his voice for somebody to come and tell him why the hell he was being starved to death and on whose orders. The footsteps came nearer and in the greenish gaslight through the opened spyhole he saw two white-faced Tommies who gaped at him in apparent terror and ran away. He set up an even louder clamour at the door, yelling at the top of his healthy lungs, and at last he heard the sound of boots again on the landing. Several pairs: he could not imagine why so many should be required to attend to one naked prisoner. A key rasped in the lock and the door swung open. The original pair of Tommies were standing as far back as they could get, against the opposite wall. An officer among the group asked him who he was, and raised small arched eyebrows when he got the answer, 'Irish prisoner.'

'Why are you in this cell?'

The prisoner lost his head then and raved with his dry damaged mouth that made his voice sound to him like rattling peas in a box. About how he found it a pleasant place to spend a summer's day, and how much better it would be if they hadn't taken his clothes away and if he had been given the usual generous rations or even allowed water. About the fires of hell and the Empire and what Captain Allen could do with his lousy paper and what Mitchel thought of British justice and a lot more.

The small neat officer remained superior and impassive. 'I understand how you feel, young man. I'll have this strange matter investigated. Return this prisoner to his block, men, and see that his clothes are returned and that he is fed a good meal immediately.'

'Yes, sir.'

'And you, Brown, ask Captain Allen to be good enough to come to my quarters.'

'Very good, sir.'

Nothing was ever the same again. The letters from his family which were put all together with another letter into his hand were as good to get as that first meal of his new life. Next day they gave him a thick writing pad, a couple of N pens and a bottle of Stephen's ink. The second letter he wrote, after the one home, was to Frances Montgomery.

'The feel of a pen between my fingers again is even better than I knew it would be, and it's a pleasure to be able to thank you at last for your letter and for coming to see me. The contents of the parcel were delicious and most welcome but next time it will be enough just to see you. You say your eldest sister Harriet will come too when she is over here – does she write poetry like you? And will she be as slow to show it to a poor devil who has his tongue hanging out for culture just now? I have asked for books, however, and I'm told my request will be forwarded to the right quarter "in due course". When I see you again I have a tale to tell will curdle your young blood. . . .'

Already he saw himself a creature of legend, Othello to the golden girl who might pity him for dangers he had passed.

Summer

SARAH'S flight had not yet been called and there was plenty of time. Her baggage checked in, she was deep now in a fashion magazine, blue-jeaned knees together and feet spread wide. She looked as carelessly uninvolved as though she were sitting on the floor of her chaotic room at home.

'Have you your passport safely stowed away?'

'Oh, Mother, you saw me do it at the check-in.'

'Did you actually *take* the Kwells? I last noticed them in your hand.'

'I actually took the Kwells. Look, relax. I have my francs and my traveller's cheques and my separate embarkation fee. I have your presents for the Vendrons (whenever I see them) and twenty changes of socks. It's not my first flight and I haven't failed my entire exam, just Structures like everybody else. I won't jump out of the plane as we take off and I won't crunch up all the travel pills. I won't die of dysentery and I'm unlikely to fall into the hands of a really competent rapist. You should know by now I'm better able to take care of myself than you are and I'm delirious to be escaping. There, they're calling my flight. Number 8 gate.'

Magazine tucked into the big canvas shoulder-bag, she stood tall and smiling down at Emily, clean black hair falling around her narrow face, eyes already away and somewhere else. On the escalator she bent and laid her cheek, moist and cool as a fruit, against Emily's.

'There isn't anywhere in the world I'd rather be going. Your fault. You made me a Francophile before I left my pram. You taught me "Frère Jacques" when you should have been teaching me ABC. You exchanged me for a Vendron at the tender age of twelve and I've never been more terrified in my *life* than on that first plane flying off alone into the unknown.'

'You were being met at Le Bourget.'

'Yes, but I didn't believe it. I didn't believe I'd live so long, and I wanted to howl like an infant and beg you to call it all off and let me live shamefully ever after.'

'You looked so cool,' Emily remembered. She had believed all the turmoil was inside herself. The forlornness of the school blazer. The smallness of Sarah as she had stumped across the tarmac, handgrip held in both arms like a puppy. Yet a few minutes previously she had kissed them coldly goodbye, exchanged a few giggling jokes with her friends who had stayed the night to be in time to see her off. All of eight years ago.

'Tell Denis when he gets back,' she said carefully at the gate. 'Tell him I said goodbye.' At the age of three Sarah had called her mother Emily but had reverted soon afterwards to custom. Her father had always remained Denis. 'Tell him thanks for the money and I'll write – well, some time. Tell him, won't you?'

'I'll tell him. And I hope the job turns out to be interesting. I wouldn't mind being in your shoes myself.'

'Why don't you come?' Eyes wide open in the hard-worked pale face, Sarah really seemed to mean it.

'Don't be silly. Give the Vendrons my love – especially Nathalie.'

'Of course, though I may not see much of them. Thanks for the lift, Mother, and the money and everything. And I will write – promise.'

'Ask them over for Christmas if they'd like to come.'

'Perhaps. But you know their position about the grand-mother. Goodbye Mother.'

'Goodbye, love. Bon voyage.' They kissed briefly.

Due to the new security regulations you couldn't go any

further, but by good fortune she caught sight of Sarah ten
minutes afterwards, swinging long-legged across the tarmac,
cheese-cloth smock about to take off by itself, it seemed, in
the strong wind. Sarah was among the tallest of the hurrying
passengers and there was about her an air of joyful freedom,
from study, from Dublin, naturally from home. The small
squat creature in the school blazer had gone bravely to her
doom. In one sense she had never come back.

Denis had stood too and watched the plane take off that
first time, a great menacing bird with flames at its tail. They
had not admitted to feeling sick with worry, but Denis had
taken her hand and squeezed it fiercely. She stood alone now
on the balcony waiting for take-off. The warm wind got
inside her cotton dress, lifting it free, as she made her ritual
wordless prayer for a safe arrival. Sarah was beyond her care
now, a woman with the right to the wrong decisions so long
as they were her own. She imagined the pale bony face tilted
back in the seat, the capable bony hands fixing the seat belt,
hands that could sketch, paint, make detailed plans for
houses she might never build, cook, sew, and no doubt make
love.

The plane was ready now. The crew had gone aboard and
now the pilot mounted the steps with a nod of thanks to the
men who had fuelled his engines. Sarah was in the care of
other people. For ever now. Emily watched the flames, saw
the plane which had taxied toy-like around the runway
shudder into flight and climb steeply into a grey June sky.
She waved as Sarah was perhaps invisibly waving. Bon
voyage.

Brown-stained fingers had pressed into her arm that first
time. 'She's beginning her independence. Already detached
from us, already chatting to strangers on either side of her.
She's safe and happy and being met at Le Bourget. She
doesn't even remember that we exist any more. Come and
have a drink.'

Shakily they had drunk without words to Sarah's safety,
Sarah's happiness, Sarah's proficiency at French. The two

friends with school blazers like Sarah's had sucked their
coke warily through straws, a little lost now that Sarah was
gone. At home in the suddenly empty house she and Denis
had made urgent love before he went to work, one of the
few completely spontaneous occasions she could remember.
It had ended in laughter because the cat had been under the
bed and squawked at the rustling springs before leaping
out onto the window sill. Sunshine through the open
window. The blinking black cat. A lawnmower whirring
somewhere. I love you.

On the way home from the airport she dropped in on
friends who (she had forgotten) were away on holiday. She
spent an hour at a deplorable annual Academy exhibition in
the National Gallery and had lunch there; a wandering
afternoon in town followed. Twice she went into a public
phone box and stood irresolute, the phone poised. When
you didn't ring I thought perhaps you were ill again so I
decided to check. How are you? No. It was over. She put
back the receiver, preferring not to hear that cautious voice
inventing the customary lies. It had been good and it was
over and no harm done unless she made a fool of herself
now. During a heavy shower she went into a cinema and
stayed although she had seen the film before. It hadn't been
worth anybody's time in the first place. She had another
cup of coffee somewhere else and finally home could not be
put off any longer. There was a letter on the kitchen table.

Emily, I'm unlikely to be back early. Hope Sarah went
off OK and that she didn't forget anything vital. Thanks
for the salmon I found in the fridge. I've somehow
remembered to order a pint less milk for tomorrow but
I could find no food for the cat. You should turn in
early after all the rush of getting Sarah off. Try this
Lionel Davidson – I liked it. D.

The note was under the paperback. It was half past eleven
and still not quite dark in the garden. A warm breath of

fading hawthorn came through the open window. She saw herself reflected in the glass, the note from Denis in one hand, his book in the other. This was the time Sarah would sometimes come running along the hall upstairs when she'd let herself in after the last bus. They would make coffee in the kitchen and turn over the news of the day. Jer and Catherine had broken it off again. Fergus had walked out on the parents and was sleeping rough in Stephen's Green. His old dear had recently started to open his letters and sniff around for drugs. She was too stupid to know that what she ought to be sniffing around for was bombs.

The old cat rubbed against Emily's ankles, bundled clumsily across the tiles to the empty bowl and back again to her ankles. Denis had been right – there *was* no cat food in the fridge. She had forgotten to get it at the butcher's yesterday. Maybe a saucer of milk would do. No. The furry collision with her ankles began all over again, a rasping of the tongue against her bare flesh, the clumsy journey back again to the milk-filled bowl. So far the creature was not howling; that would come later. Sighing, she fetched a slice of bacon from the fridge and cut it up with the kitchen scissors but that too was rejected, so there was only one thing to do. Hurriedly she gathered into a saucepan a heap of unpicked chicken bones. Since they had been reserved for soup anyway there was nothing to lose by simmering them now instead of tomorrow and there was supper to gain for the cat who knew this routine and had now given up demanding instant food. It sat at her elbow as she opened the book, making its wheezy attempt at purring.

Tired of the sound, she wandered upstairs to run a bath. Idly stepping into Sarah's room while the bath filled, she saw herself once again reflected in the blank window above the dark garden and because she didn't like what she saw she quickly pulled across the curtains. The room smelled more than ever of Sarah, of youth. Yellow lamplight showed her the chaotic disorder, maddening when Sarah was at home, childlike and touching now that she was gone.

Rejected garments for the suitcase overflowed from the open chest of drawers, littered the bed, joined a jumble on the floor of text books, sketch books, hair rollers, paper patterns, snippets of the new summer frocks she had made in the last few days, a half-eaten Mars bar and an unused tampon. The window seat was completely obscured by similar litter including shoes, boots and sandals as though they had been deliberately laid out the way a child lays out coloured sweets for selection. Compulsively Emily began to make order, interrupting the job once to turn off the bath water, then returning to sift, discard or rearrange the litter of Sarah's life.

'*Soyez réaliste,*' she had written across the cover of a big sketch book, '*demandez l'impossible.*' Not only did Sarah ask the impossible but sometimes she did it. It was during the week before one of her examinations that she had made a summer dress for Emily's birthday. No snippet of cotton had appeared anywhere to suggest what was to come, no piece of paper pattern had been left to give the game away. A blue cotton dress perfectly finished to the last detail and a perfect fit had been dumped one morning into her arms before Sarah banged the door and raced away to a lecture for which she was already late.

Inside a college magazine called *Structures* there was a sheet of paper that drifted free as Emily gathered all the magazines together:

> Arm-strapped together we watched up west
> The blood of murdered day breaking night's rest.

Motorbikes. The boy whose fledgling effort this was used to come surrounded by them as Aengus was by birds. He didn't own a motorbike but he collected friends who did. That summer motorbikes crowded for ever on the bare patch they had made under the trees. Indoors Simon and Garfunkel and the buzz of voices after school, Sarah's room overflowing onto the stairs. A pong of Gauloises or perhaps pot. Coffee and 'Bridge Over Troubled Waters'. Shouts of laughter. Always more boys than girls. The one who wrote the poem also fed the cat while they were away on that last family holiday. Because he loved cats he had come in every day for a month and he had sent on selected post also. The house had not felt empty when they came home. He was a big brown curly bear of a boy – what was his name? Ruairí. He had left a note with the month's bills on the kitchen table.

Ah ah! Don't look. One suspects a predominance of canondal mordentary apperatures. Anyway they all arrived too late to send on except 2 which were filed in my impeccable system under W for 'Where do I put these?' Céad mile fáilte (approx equal to 400 new fáiltes) Cheers. Ruairí.

The note fluttered out with the poem and the closing fragment of a letter. 'But me no goodbyes. Parting is such sweet whatyacallit. Brightness falls into the lair. Give you good morrow. Your sleepless step-in wolf.'

He was dead two years now, found a tangle of bones and burnt metal when he crashed a borrowed motorbike one Saturday night on the Bray Road. These pages Sarah had kept together were evidently a memorial collection. But me no goodbyes. Parting is such sweet whatyacallit.

Sarah's sheets were rumpled but changing them would have seemed like rejection. They smelled of lemon soap and patchouli and made a warmer bed than the one upstairs. After a bath she was reading Sarah's Tolkien and half asleep when a key turned in the hall door. Switching off the light was instinctive but sleep was now far away. A smell of burnt bones crept up from the kitchen and already the heavy foot-steps of Denis were sounding from that direction. He would find a starving beast and a ruin of spoiled supper. She began to laugh with hysterical guilt and then put her head under the clothes to stifle the sound. Faintly she could hear the

yowls of the cat in panic-stricken welcome and her mind
followed Denis's movements. First things first. He would
switch off the cooker. Then open windows and doors wide.
Then comfort the afflicted animal. Most probably he would
make such a determined effort that he would find the cat
something apart from the piece of uncooked salmon in the
fridge. She had one impulse to go down and make abject
apologies but in a little while this impulse was completely
conquered. Tomorrow would be time enough.

She woke next morning to a silent house and sun flooding
through the curtains. The house felt empty, which was
impossible. Downstairs, nevertheless, it was empty, with a
note on the kitchen table to prove it.

Emily, I'm afraid you forgot the chicken bones again.
Cleared up as best I could and found a tin of cat food
out in the car – dating from that camping holiday years
ago, I have no doubt. It seemed quite fresh however
and the cat didn't complain. You were sleeping so
soundly I didn't like to waken you to let you know I
must put in a few hours work to make up for a broken
day yesterday when I had to see Henderson. Appoint-
ment with the Minister on Monday morning and
practically no background data prepared. May not get
home for lunch so don't wait. D.

Working on Sundays was something new but then his
partner was on holiday. If Denis could find the slightest
excuse for extra work he wouldn't hesitate. She wanted to
ring him and apologise, say something to hear him laugh.
But there was nobody on the switchboard. Even if she drove
into the main entrance the office block would be closed to
everybody who hadn't a private key – he might as well be
on the moon.

She opened the windows wide and hoped the reek of
burnt bones would go away in the sunshine. Leaning out on
the window sill she sniffed the morning. Hawthorn still, and

wild garlic, and a hint of tom cats. In a moment there was the creak of a basket behind her and the huge woolly creature walked stiff-legged across the tiles. Its fur in the sunlight was a decayed brownish black, profuse because of remote Persian ancestry. Its golden goat's eyes avoided her when it lumbered up on the window sill. Nevertheless it sat companionably by her elbow and yawned, diffusing its old cat smell.

Mechanically she stroked it, and its strange rattling purr grew louder.

It was so old that it had curled up beside Sarah in the cot, guarding her from wasps in summer and from boredom at all times. Its name was Simpkin and Denis claimed that some vital mechanism (like the gizzard of a goose) had stopped working inside so that the cat had no way of dealing with the accumulation of fur swallowed during its ablutions. That is, it had one way, recently devised. Sometimes Emily would find a ball of fur and mucus near its basket on the tiles and for a few days it would sound less wheezy before the fur built up again. Eventually she supposed it would choke and then they could keep a dog instead.

It licked her wrist now with a rasping tongue before lumbering over the window sill into the garden. All old creatures, animal and human, move in the same way. Simpkin in bright incongruous sunshine looked more than somewhat like Aunt Harry. It was Sunday. 'Just as soon as I pack Sarah off I'll be over to see you,' she remembered saying. Sarah was wakening up in Paris or already sitting on the balcony, drinking café au lait out of a big bowl, apricot jam heaped into a split roll on her plate. There isn't anywhere in the world I'd rather be going, Sarah had said. But this was Dublin and today was Harry's day. Turning on her heel to make coffee, Emily found herself sliding on the tiles and bent down to see why. The ball of mucus and fur had been silently left at her feet, like an offering.

Terminus

THERE was a rule at St Elizabeth's that nobody going in must leave the door open, even if another caller was on his way up the steps. It was not to prevent the escape of the inmates, since the old ladies were free to come and go as they pleased. Nevertheless it was a rule which nobody ever broke. Emily found the door about to shut in her face just as she reached the top step and she put out a hand to stop it. Her fingertips were grazed by the brass handle and one fingernail broke but the door banged shut anyway. She stood listening to the dragging walk of the tiny polio lady whose job it was to open the door. Miss Black had brittle bird bones, golden hair and a doll's tiny smile. Her wrist was strapped up again.

'Nothing to worry about, dear. I slipped on my way in to Mass. Just a little greenstick fracture like last time. We are a Little Crusty today, I fear.' When she used the first person plural she meant Aunt Harry. 'Waiting for you, despite advice, since early morning, I'm afraid, dear. Wouldn't come in for coffee for fear she'd miss you. We had a job to get her to take any lunch.'

'Oh dear.'

'Don't worry, my dear, she's perfectly well again. She'll cheer up when she sees you.'

'Thank you for letting me in, Miss Black. I hope your wrist will be OK soon.'

'Please God. Tell Auntie I was asking for her.'

Baffled by this request, Emily passed by the lift entrance

and ran upstairs. On every landing there were pots of flowers resting on tall pot stands which came from a hundred former residences. Sometimes there were burnished mahogany hall chairs beside them as though one might want to sit down and admire the growth. Occasionally an old lady, rightly distrustful of the lift, went down a flight of stairs backwards, holding the rail with both hands, drawing both slippered feet together on each step. Frequently a greeting evoked no response except a blank stare, but sometimes it did.

'June is treacherous, I always say,' one of the old ladies said. 'You should always wrap up well going out. Easier to catch a cold in June than to cure it, I always say.'

'Of course,' Emily agreed. 'Have you had your holidays yet?'

'Sister Camillus is waiting for me,' the old lady said with finality. 'Mustn't keep her.'

She continued her crablike progress downstairs and Emily ran up the remaining two flights of stairs to Harry. Her aunt was sitting in the plant-filled room with hat and coat on, swollen knuckles closed over the bulldog handle of her walking stick, massively displeased.

'I thought you'd never come, Emily. I should have thought you'd remember that today being the day before tomorrow, which is the twelfth, I'd want to be taken to the cemetery. Now half the afternoon is gone already.'

'It's only half past three, Aunt. How are you?' Emily forced herself to kiss the wrinkled powdery paper that was the old face under a black straw hat with cherries on it. But Harry struggled firmly up with the aid of her stick.

'We've got no time to waste now, Emmy, now that you are here. Did you tell Sarah to have a Mass said in Lourdes for poor Richard as I told you?'

'Sarah has gone to Paris, Aunt Harry. It's further from Lourdes than London is from here. She won't be going anywhere near Lourdes.'

'You mean to say the child has gone *again* to France and

won't be near Lourdes this time either? Oh well, I dare say she can't be blamed for that. She was taught no ritual of piety any more than *you* were. If only things had been different. . . .'

This crazy dream Emily had been listening to since childhood. It was what had frequently driven her away during school holidays with this aunt, who had moved from Ballsbridge to a house near the Phoenix Park at that stage. There used to be dolls in the Edwardian bedroom. A baby doll dressed in baby clothes that had once been Emily's lay smirking on the bed. If only things had been different. . . . It meant if only God had not had that temporary aberration which made Him bestow children on a frivolous younger sister rather than on Harry herself. It meant if only she, Harriet, had not had to spend her youth in the services of a thankless family, if only she had not had to look after her own dear mother until that apparently immortal old lady died at last at the age of eighty-five. It meant if only she and Richard had not had to wait so long to get married.

'Don't think I ever blamed dear Fanny for getting married before me, although some might,' Harry was saying handsomely as she crawled along the polished corridor with the aid of her stick and Emily's arm. 'Did I lock the door, dear? Go back and see.'

'You locked it, Aunt, and put the key in your bag.'

'You'd be there and back before I'd find it in my bag. Go back and see did I lock the door, Emmy.'

Emily left the old lady holding on to the handrail with which all the passages in this place were provided. On the way back she stopped to talk to another resident. One had to be careful to remember that they were residents, not inmates.

'Such a lovely day,' Miss Furlong smiled. 'You should take Auntie to the seaside – she'd like that.'

'How is your arm?' Emily enquired.

'Old bones mend slowly – we have to expect that. It's perfectly all right if I don't put too much weight on it. I have to remember, for instance, not to lift up my bag with my right hand.'

'You should empty as much as you can out of your bag,' Emily advised, and then remembered that handbags as heavy as suitcases were usual here. You could never be quite sure of servants these days, the residents told one another. Just as Emily was moving off she had to answer a polite enquiry about Sarah. It turned out that Miss Furlong had been to Paris once as a girl.

Harry was furious when her niece got back. 'Standing is the worst possible thing for my legs. You should know that. And that woman is only looking for information. You should ignore her. Her father was a second-class booking clerk in Westland Row station. I get on well with everybody, of course – even her – but there's no need for you to pay the slightest attention to her. She has a battalion of nephews and nieces coming to visit her. I only have you. Did I lock my door properly, dear? Did you pull it *firmly* to make sure?'

'Yes, you locked your door properly, Aunt.'

They resumed the slow crawl to the lift at the bottom of the corridor. Some of the doors were open on either side, revealing the odd figure bundled into a dressing gown, examining the sun through closed windows. Sometimes an old lady came out smiling to wish Harry a pleasant outing but it was usually Emily who answered for her.

The lift was ultra-modern in design and something of a hazard. You had to step fairly smartly in as soon as the doors opened, otherwise they closed automatically and crushed you. The alternative (which of course Harry had discovered) was to press an emergency button which flashed red alerts all along the four storeys and was intended to bring prompt aid to somebody who had passed out in the lift or been otherwise stricken. Emily attempted to help the old lady firmly into the lift but Harry would have none of it.

'Press the emergency button, dear.'

'But really, Aunt, it is intended for emergencies.' The lift gate snapped shut and the lift sailed away.

'It isn't even as if you were on *time* to begin with,' Harry said irritably. 'I was waiting fully dressed for half an hour. Not to speak of this morning. It's really too bad of you in view of the occasion – I have flowers to buy as you well know.'

Without speaking Emily pressed the button again as soon as she heard the lift halt and it returned at the same time as a nurse about to begin her half-day off. No emergency button this time. Harry allowed herself to be hauled smartly into the lift by the nurse and Emily and then stood panting between them, straightening the cherries on her hat.

'Off for the day, Mrs Reidy?' the nurse said brightly. 'Such a lovely day you have for it.'

'I'm not off to amuse myself, nurse, I assure you. My dear husband will be twelve years at rest tomorrow and I've never missed an anniversary even if it has to be the day before because Emily is so often busy on the right day. But my niece has a family to take care of, you know – we mustn't grumble.'

'How many children?' the nurse smiled.

'Just one.' A lifetime of apology to perfect strangers for that – why?

'Very well organised,' said the nurse archly. 'I must run – excuse me. Have a lovely day, Mrs Reidy.' The girl skipped out nimbly for fear of losing any more of her half-day and Harry held herself in readiness for the major enterprise of dismounting, as from a horse. Emily attempted to manoeuvre her neatly into the hall but she would have none of it. Under the shiny black straw her old dry face crumpled in reproach.

'Press the emergency button, dear.'

'Honestly I don't think you should,' Emily began again, worried, just as the gates closed automatically. Somebody pressed the button on another floor and the lift glided instantly up, third-floor button flashing.

'Now see what happens when you don't do as you are told – what could be simpler than the request to press a button? It isn't as though you were even on *time*. . . .'

The third-floor passenger was a young housemaid Emily had often seen polishing tiles. 'This lift,' said Harry coldly, 'is for the use of residents and nursing staff. You're young enough at all events to use the stairs – much better for your figure too.'

The small fat housemaid looked at Harry with under-standable loathing but said nothing. Emily passed a pacifying remark about the weather which nobody answered. On the first landing two other residents were waiting in hats and coats to enter.

'How are you, dear?' the one in the pink hat said to Harry. 'I always say to Matron how wonderful it is the way you keep so cheerful with the poor rheumatism and everything.'

'Mustn't complain,' Harry said briskly to Emily's astonish-ment. 'Plenty worse off than I am. This is my niece, Mrs Ryan. Miss Allingham, Emily.'

'Hello, Miss Allingham.'

'How do you do, dear? You should take Auntie away home to live with you – she'd like that much better.' The sudden-ness of this took Emily's breath away, and it was Harry who answered.

'My niece is much too busy with her husband and family, Miss Allingham. You wouldn't know anything about the difficulties of running a home, never having married. We must be reasonable.'

The lift stopped just as the unruffled Miss Allingham asked, 'How many children, dear?'

'A daughter,' Emily said, looking her straight in the eye, and Miss Allingham bubbled. 'How nice – one little girl. Have a nice afternoon now, Mrs Reidy, and take care of yourself.'

Before emerging from the lift Miss Allingham pressed the emergency button and Harry beamed her thanks for this civility. With crablike slowness she was the last to cross the threshold of the lift. Emily offered to take the black bag (which weighed about half a stone) but Harry shook her head and allowed the bag to weigh her down on one side as she scratched along with the stick in her other hand. When she was safely out in the hall Emily released the emergency button and the lift snapped shut as Harry rapped with her stick on the door of the little office. Miss Black appeared with the suddenness of a mechanical doll which tells the weather.

'Would you be good enough to inform them in the kitchen I won't be in to tea?'

'With pleasure, Mrs Reidy. Have a lovely time, dear.'

Getting Harry down the steps looked like taking half an hour and it occurred to Emily that the old lady might be faster on her own. She had, after all, the railings to support her.

'If you give me that heavy bag and your stick I'll bring the car right to the bottom of the steps – there was no parking any nearer when I arrived.'

'What about *that* space?' Harry wanted to know, stopping and pointing with the stick she refused to surrender. 'That's always free. Why couldn't you have parked there in the first place?'

'Because it says Ambulance, Aunt, to warn motorists off. It *must* be kept free, naturally.'

'Nonsense,' the old lady said firmly. 'No ambulance ever comes here – why should it? This is not a hospital.'

Emily wanted suddenly to shout: 'What does come over and over again is the hearse – ambulance is a euphemism,' but she held her tongue and went to bring around the car. When she returned Harry was standing at the foot of the steps tilted to one side like an old crow in the wind, gently swaying. This time Emily succeeded in detaching her from both stick and handbag, leaving her to clutch the railings while these belongings were thrown onto the back seat. Next came the business of getting the old lady into the car. Harry dithered as always like a reluctant swimmer before trusting herself to make the effort necessary to enter the car. Presumably her arthritic knees felt as unsteady as she looked at the prospect of this unfamiliar down-movement; possibly she might be in considerable pain. At last she swayed again and dipped suddenly into the front passenger seat, straw hat askew, gnarled body shuddering. Only the coat remained to be bundled into the car after her. Emily straightened her carefully as though she were a baby in a pram.

'Mind your elbow now, Aunt Harry. Try and sit upright. That's it.' She slammed the door and ran around to the driving seat. 'OK Aunt Harry?'

'All right,' Harry said, 'only it's nearly time for us to be coming back. Hurry on now, dear, to the florist. That's our first stop – but listen, isn't it a pity it's Sunday, dear? If it was any other day, you could take me to the dry cleaner's to collect my coat and skirt. It should have been ready yesterday – that's the place we're passing now.'

'It's a clearway on weekdays,' Emily explained, trying to be patient. 'I'd be fined if I stopped there.'

'Then I don't know how the taxi-man always manages to do it.'

'Neither do I!'

'Never mind, dear, it's not important. We must get on and pick up the flowers. Full steam ahead.'

The florist was one of those to be found near the walls of any cemetery. It opened not only on Sundays but on Christmas Day as well. One year Emily had been persuaded to take her aunt here for the purpose of laying a wreath of holly on Richard's grave and it had taken an hour, driving bumper to bumper along the cemetery paths.

Richard lay with his feet to the city and his head to the hills. Each year it was harder to find him as the cemetery became more and more like a housing estate growing up around him. Harry hugged the pot of rusty chrysanthemums and offered advice.

'I remember that nice headstone with the Sacred Heart. Turn left, dear. Richard's place is at the bottom of that little path.'

'We made that mistake last year, Aunt – don't you remember?'

'Very well, it's the *next* left turn. I distinctly remember.'

The sun was low over the green hillside when Richard's grave was found at last. Emily took the pot of flowers and laid it on a tombstone while she helped Harry out. From the recesses of the black bag a trowel had magically appeared. 'Just to tidy him up for the occasion,' Harry explained. 'You won't mind helping me, dear?'

Richard's place had sprouted green life since this time last year, despite the marble chips, but it was customary to kneel down and pray before commenting on it. It took five minutes to get Harry onto her knees, and ten to get her up again. The customary tears were wiped angrily away with a black net glove.

'People are so *dishonest* nowadays – how could that man take good money for keeping the grave clean when it's only too obvious he never goes near it? At all events it won't take you long, dear. This is a very sharp little trowel. There is no point whatever in putting flowers on a grave which looks so dreadfully shabby.'

She leaned on her stick as Emily did the weeding. Once she took off her glasses to see if any sprouts had been forgotten. Finally she was satisfied. 'Now the pot of flowers, dear. No, not there. Nearer to his head. You remember how fond of chrysanthemums poor Uncle Richard always was? I do hope at least that man will keep them watered. We must knock at the office on the way out to remind him.'

Mercifully the office was shut and the last visitors were straggling out when they reached the gates. 'We'll wait until he comes to lock up, dear. He *must* lock the gates, I should imagine.'

'If we wait we'll be too late for afternoon tea at the hotel. And you must be tired.'

'Well, so I am. But I have never been one to pander to self-indulgence when something needs to be done.'

In a flash that made her tremble on the edge of revelation, Emily heard across the years her own mother's mocking laugh as she mimicked her tiresome eldest sister. Harry was

fifteen years older – already old, it seemed, when Emily's
mother had been a wilful schoolgirl (the best-looking of that
family) and Emily heard her lazy laugh now, saw the
cigarette ash crumbling from the tip of a long amber holder
and drifting finally down onto a floppy tussore blouse the
colour of country butter. 'Poor old Sister Harry. Suffered
dreadfully from sanctimonious attacks whenever she lost a
man.' Fanny's newly bobbed hair was soft and blowaway.
She smelled as always of Aimant de Coty. Her eyes neither
green nor blue, had amber flecks in them like the cigarette
holder.

'You can *write* to the grave-keeper,' Emily suggested.
'They probably pay more attention to a letter.'

'Very well, dear, you may be right. And that reminds me.
I need more notepaper next time you're coming – unless we
could get it now.'

'Perhaps after tea,' Emily said firmly.

Harry was dissatisfied with the service and with the
strength of the beverage. 'As you know I always liked tea
you could trot a mouse on, dear. So did poor Richard. At
home in your own place you make a very nice cup of tea.'

'Denis is away just now on business and as you know
Sarah is away too. It's more cheerful here – so much nearer
for you too. Have a scone, Aunt – they look homemade and
delicious.'

With careful management, each word weighed before
being uttered, Emily produced an atmosphere of relaxation
at last. There was a bad moment when it was discovered
there was no fruitcake or anything sweeter to follow the
scones, but this was overcome later by the purchase of mint
chocolates in the lounge. All seemed to be well for the return
to St Elizabeth's. But all was not well.

'Poor Richard was so fond of these lovely summer evenings – remember how you used to come driving with us as a
little girl after tea? He specially loved Enniskerry, but if we
were as late as this we often just went to Chapelizod through
the Phoenix Park.'

'Oh yes, I remember.' There was no help for it. 'Maybe you'd like to come for a little drive along the Liffey Valley now before we go back?'

'That would be lovely, dear. Miss Black will love to hear about it. She never goes out herself, poor thing.'

Chapelizod was lapped in green light and the river was noisy and full. Later Emily pulled in to the side of the leafy road.

'Poor Mother used to take us out here to the Strawberry Beds,' Harry remembered. 'That was before her poor legs got bad after Dan was born. For threepence you could eat all the strawberries and cream you could hold and the boys often accounted for four bowls each, I declare. Not your mama, and I, of course. Fanny and I used to laugh at the boys disgracing themselves. The last time we came was the summer before the war – 1913, that would be. Fanny wore a blue and white cotton that I made for her and mine was red. That dress was all stained with strawberry juice before the end of the evening but you couldn't tell because of the colour. Fanny's was a perfect disgrace going home on the side-car. I remember she laughed and said it wasn't fair – I'd spilled just as much strawberry juice as she had.'

'Would you like a little walk down by the river now, Aunt? It's so warm and still.'

'No dear, it's lovely just sitting here and looking at it. Poor Richard and I used to come here on his motorcycle before you were born – before Fanny got married, even.'

'You were engaged to Richard for a long time, weren't you?' That was a safe question. Harry could never repeat the story too often.

'Oh yes. Young people nowadays wouldn't believe it. You and Denis were only engaged for three months, isn't that so? If you had known one another a little better maybe there wouldn't be so many business trips now. But Richard and I were like brother and sister for years because we were both so devoted to Mother. Poor Mother came to depend on me you see. Richard was quite content to come and sit with us in the evenings and chat. Sometimes of course she'd

make us go out and then we'd often come here. Of course
she had Father to look after her but he was so often out
meddling with the car. Once – did I ever tell you, I wonder? –
we bought a lovely inlaid mahogany bedroom suite at a sale
in Arnott's and then we had to have it stored. It was costing
us so much in the end that we had to sell it after ten years.
We were fifteen years engaged to be married, Richard and I,
and I was often afraid he'd marry somebody else. But
Richard wasn't that kind. When we got married at last after
Mother died I knew it was all worth while – thirty-three
years of perfect happiness.'

'How old were you at the time of the wedding?'

'Let me see – I wasn't young, of course. Late thirties, I
should think.' Out of the depths of family folklore Emily
suddenly remembered: Harriet had been forty-six and
Richard forty. 'I often think it was God did it that we
didn't have any family. Children are so often not good to
their parents when they get on in life – isn't that so? And I
have you, after all, dear. Richard always regarded you as a
daughter, you know. He often said he couldn't have been
fonder of you if you had been our own, and not dear Fanny's.'

Richard had been a little too fond of her the summer she
was twelve. She remembered the breathless hot evenings and
the smell of cut grass and the avuncular teasings in the
garden that once or twice had ended in touches that were
not avuncular at all and had to be shaken off with baffled
energy. Later she remembered his small warm brown eyes
silently asking her not to say anything about it; as though
she could ever find the words even if she'd wanted to tell
Harry. Now she thought of him with pity and affection,
remembering the legend she had scratched away the moss
from with her trowel: Richard Albert Reidy, LL.B., beloved
husband of Harriet, born Dublin 16th May 1890, died 12th
June 1963. R.I.P.

The inscription took up only half the tombstone, the rest
being reserved for Harriet who in due course would be
placed on top of him.

'Your dear mother introduced us, you know,' Harriet said. 'Brought him home to tea one evening from the office. Later they went to see *Naughty Marietta* at the Gaiety and wanted to bring me too. But I couldn't leave poor Mother – Fanny should have known that if she wasn't such a flipperty gibbet. Later still, of course, Richard came to see *me*. He wasn't really Fanny's type at all. Her next young man was more her own kind. That was your own dear father, as you know.'

'I didn't know the sequence, actually.'

'Oh yes, he was much more Fanny's type – flighty, a little, you know, fond of politics and theatricals and that sort of thing. God be good to them both now and to poor Richard and Mother and poor Dan. Sometimes I feel they are the lucky ones, all together up there now. But I must soldier along so long as God wills it. What time is it, Emily? Drive me back then, dear. I've had quite enough airing for one day. I nearly said "Drive me home", but of course I have no home now nor anyone who cares enough to give me a home. But God's will be done. We never got the notepaper, Emmy.'

'Don't worry, I'll bring it to you next time, Aunt.'

Labouring up the steps of St Elizabeth's, Harry reminded her of the notepaper again. 'And don't be late next time, dear, as you were today. But thank you at all events for a most pleasant afternoon. Next time we'll collect the coat and skirt at the cleaner's so don't make it a Sunday.'

Emily forced herself once again to kiss the powdered paper cheeks before handing Harry over to Miss Black. 'See you Saturday then, Aunt.'

'God bless you. And drive carefully across the city, Emmy.'

Emily drew in a deep breath as the stained-glass door closed. She sucked her broken fingernail on the way back to the car. She had forgotten once again to verify that her grandmother had been called Emily which would be why the dead Fanny had called *her* Emily. Next week, perhaps.

A Cut Above the Rest

I SUPPOSE in a way you could say I am my mother's justification, being the one who made it into the overdraft belt, those parts of inner or scenic outer suburbia where the mere lack of cash doesn't matter, has never mattered. I think often of her careful stagemanagement of my future, and I can't help smiling because I never really got away. No matter how rich I have ever temporarily felt, I can't spend money on, let's say, the trimmings of a meal. I can buy wine but never the best cut of smoked salmon for a starter: I buy salmon tails and bury them in what is known as good presentation. I buy slightly-flawed best bed linen at annual sales but I can never splurge on, say, really beautiful bath towels or cut flowers.

I think poor, as a wealthy Jew whose father pushed a scrap-cart said to me once. And this is strange, because the rule of our house at home was that we thought rich. That was what set us apart from our neighbours in the ugly northside terrace which was near enough and similar enough to the municipal housing estate to be frequently confused with it. In fact the ambition of many of our neighbours was to be housed by the local authority for even less than what seem, in retrospect, the modest private rentals of those days when only the rich bought their own houses. Most people rented houses big or small, and it was the ambition of my mother to rent a bigger house in a more acceptable district which would land us in debt but do us justice.

All the arguments I can ever remember between my happy

parents were about this. My father said that living in a stable didn't make you a horse and that this was a mixed district anyway. What about the Carters? The Carters, like ourselves, didn't quite belong. Mr Carter worked in advertising and Mrs Carter gave piano lessons. It was not the sort of house from which you got the smell of coddle or the sounds of a drunken brawl on a Saturday night. They even had two Victorian urns filled with geraniums on either side of the tiny hall door. The urns were a nuisance because you had to edge in sideways between them and if Mrs Carter had had a baby and therefore a pram, the whole thing would have become impossible. But like ourselves (once my small brother grew a bit) there was no baby in that house. They had two small boys like ours and they had Annette who was my friend for a while. The other houses in the street were seldom without a pram in the hall and a raft of children tearing the garden to shreds or spilling over into the street with their games.

I had music lessons from Mrs Carter and I also practised there because, as my mother said, she hadn't yet found exactly the right piano for us. Exactly the right piano for us was, I presume, a secondhand one costing about a fiver. A good new piano cost about forty pounds then, but it was no further away from us in terms of attainability than a fiver. Fivers were needed for a new suit for my father when his position as salesman would have been jeopardised by more mending. Fivers were needed to pay school fees and electricity bills and sometimes to give a really splendid present to my aunt Harriet – like a wireless set, for instance, which my father got (as he could get most things except pianos) at 'the right price'. So long as she could give the odd splendid present to her elder sister, my mother never felt inferior and therefore unhappy. It didn't matter that Harriet's presents to us were always of a much more modest nature. In fact that made it even better. And some day, my mother promised, some day she would find the right sort of piano for us.

What about Mrs Stapleton, my father said. Oh yes, Mrs

Stapleton. She was elderly and sad and Protestant but she
had once had a son. He was a poet, and the glory of his
career filled the walls of the little house. He had not only
been a poet but he had been connected with the Abbey
Theatre at one time, much more firmly connected than my
father who had merely played there once or twice. Roderic
Stapleton, the son's name was, and now nothing is remembered of his fame. Poetry anthologies come and go with
never a mention of him. If my father were alive he would be
quietly triumphant. He always claimed the man was only a
rhymester like himself, but more successful. More confusing
to all but the very alert. He used the language of the twilight,
the language Yeats copied from Ernest Dowson before giving
it an Irish accent. Roderic Stapleton was very fashionable at
one time because the master poet had publicly given him
his blessing. He was a kind of crown prince, good-looking,
charming, a drunk and a gambler like my uncle Dan but a
successful drunk, a successful poet, even a very successful
producer at the Abbey Theatre. His lopsided grin and the
hairstyle he copied from Yeats appealed for admiration and
indulgence from three dozen photographs on his mother's
wall. Playbills were framed and hung too, also Roderic's
conferring photograph in 1919 at Trinity, also his rugby cap.
Well, that wasn't framed, but it hung with a touchingly
boyish air of waiting till tomorrow morning on the wooden
rack in his room, which was preserved as a sort of childhood
museum, rocking horse and all.

Mrs Stapleton, poor soul, was all very well, my mother
conceded, but we mustn't lose any opportunity to look for a
better house. Meanwhile she happily painted and polished
and contrived until our abode resembled nothing so much as
a glittering doll's house. There was of course, she kept
reminding us, the house in Drumcondra, and that might be
ours one day.

Of course, the house in Drumcondra. It was a recurring
dream of my mother's to own it because however run-down
it might have become since the death of my grandmother, it

was unequivocally middle-class. It was one of a terrace of polychrome brick, set well back from the road with bay windows and tiled pathways and ornate bootscrapers and railings shaped like the ace of spades. Its Nottingham lace curtains were held back by polished metal bands and in the porch hung a huge old gas lantern which at Christmas used to be garlanded with ivy. It stood not far from the Bishop's Palace, but a bit nearer to the Tolka Cottages whose elder children used to wheel out the red-brick babies in their prams or help in the house during spring cleaning. If they proved reliable they were taken on as cook-housekeeper and 'trained' – that is, given practically no money while doing all the dirty work until some unspecified period had passed when they were judged to be 'trained'. In the early days of her marriage, my mother told me, grandmother had found her a girl from the cottages who had cycled around by Goose Green every morning to help in our house but it hadn't lasted long. Her name was Maisie Clancy, and reading between the carefully edited lines my mother gave me I gather she had told my grandmother that our house wasn't much of a cut above the Tolka Cottages, and she'd sooner work near her own place, thank you. In the end my mother was fortunate the girl left because soon afterwards she found Nanny Sheeran, but that is another story.

At the time I'm speaking of, the family in Drumcondra had dwindled to four souls locked together in what remained of a large-family interdependence. The two elder brothers of my mother were in America, one a dentist, and the other an auctioneer. The next girl was married to a sheep-farmer in Australia. The youngest brother Dan, (a barrister who never held a brief), had moved in his merry young wife from Wexford who lived in perpetual mocking conflict with the remaining unmarried sister, my aunt Evelyn, until she, poor soul, was put into a home. I am not sure at this far remove whether she was always mentally retarded or not, or whether subnormality was attributed to her by that family because she used to go out with British Auxiliaries during the

Troubles – actually be seen with them gossiping and giggling under the trees along Lower Drumcondra Road. Once she had even gone to the Volta with a sergeant from Swansea, and after this Harriet, the eldest, was detailed by my grandmother to watch Evelyn closely and report any sign of a recurrence. It was even said that the hussy had broken her mother's heart, because soon after this my grandmother apparently took to her bed with arthritis never to rise again. Harriet had left her job as a book-keeper in Lloyd, Armstrong and Frazer's to look after the invalid, and vowed she would never marry while her mother was alive. I remember seeing my grandmother dead at last like a marble statue on the high brass bed in her red bedroom surrounded by six tall candles. Her face was cold and hard like marble when I was lifted up to kiss it, and Aunt Harriet said this was because her soul was in heaven. The only other thing I remember about this was my grandfather standing with his hard hat twisting in his hands at the open doorway from which Harriet tried to hunt him on the grounds that he would only upset himself. Gentle old man though he was, he pushed her roughly aside and made for the white-draped bed where he knelt down after kissing the corpse and stayed with bent head until my mother came to take him away.

After that he came often to our house for tea and I think it was he who put it into my mother's head that the house in Drumcondra might one day be hers. Apart from Dan she was the youngest of that family and so had no possible claim on the house. But my grandfather had always liked her best. When he retired from the *Freeman's Journal* and began to spend most of every day tinkering with the two old cars in his coach-house, it was my mother who used to spend most time out there with him – she was twelve or so then, and she used to sit in the old Model T with him (which he hoped to revitalise with spare parts from the other old car) and read him her poetry.

One piece written on old jotter paper I still have – a ballad about bold Robert Emmett and his love Sarah Curran. It was probably the nearest my grandfather ever came to the fight for Irish freedom apart from interviewing revolutionaries for his newspaper but his house was always open to men on the run and it is said Michael Collins had once hidden in one of the old cars out in the back until a house to house search for him was over.

That house in a way was my house. I passed it every day cycling along the Drumcondra Road to school, to the same school where my mother and all my aunts had gone before me. I often stopped at the house for a drink of milk on my way home if the day was hot. I often took shelter there from a shower in winter. Some of the girls in school thought I lived there and I didn't correct them. Katy from Wexford, Dan's wife, was a slattern but always welcoming. Under her direction the house went steadily downhill. She had been cured of cleaning for ever as a result of one holocaust soon after she arrived as Dan's bride. That orgy of spring cleaning had ended in a bonfire out in the back garden in which had perished my grandfather's press-cutting book from his days on the *New York Herald Tribune*, all the letters he had ever written to my grandmother, and the entire family stock of baby curls, milk teeth and First Communion photographs. Now Katy never even bothered to use the sunshade and so the paint blistered and peeled on the green hall door. The door brasses which had once glistened under the old lantern grew green and mildewy. Soon even the stained glass panels became so thick with dust you could hardly make out the delicate tulip pattern from inside. Dust gathered too on the plush curtains in the hall and built up in the corners of the old red and blue carpet. A smell of tom cats and sour dishwater came up the four quarry stone steps from the kitchen and I didn't wonder that my grandfather hardly ever emerged from the coach-house at the bottom of the garden.

I suppose he must have come in to eat and sleep, but I always had to hunt him out in the garden to say hello. He would ask me about old Mother Mary Thomas in Eccles

Street and tell me what a merry young girl she had been when he was a boy. He would tell me again about the time he and some other Belvedere boys had taken part in an operetta at the Convent, or about trick-cycling in the Phoenix Park on Sunday mornings when he was a boy, or about when he interviewed the Fenian James Stephens for his newspaper in New York, or about the old days in the *Freeman's Journal* when he would battle to prevent a single word being printed against the Chief, the great Charles Stewart Parnell: sometimes he recounted these battles with his editor in detail. Or he would tell me about the first meal my grandmother had ever cooked for him when they were five years married and the girl in the kitchen ran off with a soldier who was killed in the Boer War whereupon she came back to cook for them until she married again. Her name was Nancy and she cooked the most melting bacon and cabbage you'd taste in a day's walk.

I think my grandfather must often have been hungry, but he would never hear a word spoken against the Wexford wife by my mother or anybody else. Maybe she *had* no taste for housework or cooking but she was a good wee girl, Katy, and she had a lot to put up with from the Gentleman. That was what he called my Uncle Dan, the Gentleman. And it was a poor family, he said, that couldn't support one Gentleman. He'd sit by the fire at home, eating buttered scones, and play with my two young brothers, while encouraging my mother in her dreams of owning his house. Old blue eyes lively in the brick-red face, he would say that the Gentleman would not be left unprovided for, but that Fanny, my mother, was the girl to bring the old house back to life again, the way it used to be in her mother's day, God be good to her. Later when he would drive away in the rattling old car to his spectral house where he might often have to help Katy lug the drunken Gentleman up to bed, my mother would sit up late over the fire with my father dreaming of when we would all live happily in her old home again, and of the parties we would be able to give. Half asleep in the 'return' room whose wall above my bed was open to the staircase, I would listen to her giggling and plotting and planning, and sometimes hear the futile admonition of my father: 'But Fanny, my dear, think of the upkeep, only think of what that house would cost us to run.'

Once, on an April Sunday morning I shall never forget, he had taken me to see his own old home which was very different. It was in Phibsboro, one of a square of identical small houses fronting directly onto the pavement and built towards the end of the last century for the employees of the Great Southern and Western Railway Company. He stood taller by far now than the little blue hall door of Number 16 and the sun shone on his flaming red hair with its matching bushy eyebrows. He looked proudly down at me, like a farmer showing off a particularly fine field of grain. Because it was Sunday morning, a cluster of little girls in First Communion frocks were giggling around us, wondering what we were doing there. He chaffed them and pulled the long black hair of one of them.

'You'd be Tommy Byrne's girl, now wouldn't you?'

The girl giggled and nodded her head and I felt extremely embarrassed as they all turned to gaze at me. 'I'd know you out of him in a dozen,' my father said, pleased. 'Tommy and I were boys at Knutsford together,' he explained to me as another might say, 'We were up together at Oxford.'

Before opening the door, the woman of Number 16 took a look through the parted curtains of the little front window. Her expression was not friendly, but my father gave her the full treatment in his big splendid voice.

'Bartholomew J. Mullens, madam, at your service. Forgive me the disturbance at this hour of the morning, but I wanted to show the little girl here the house where her old father grew up when all the world was young. Bliss was it in that dawn to be alive – but I don't need to tell you that.' He smiled and shook her warmly by the reluctantly offered hand and asked to whom he had the honour of speaking. She was

Mrs Noonan, she said, and my father gave a theatrical shout
of joy, to the renewed giggles of all the little girls.

'Not Mrs Andy Noonan, by all that's wonderful?' and the
loud booming of his name brought the woman's husband
out beside her into the tiny square place where coats hung
on pegs behind them and a red lamp burned to the Sacred
Heart.

'Andy, my dear fellow, after all these years,' said my
father, and Mr Noonan shouted, 'Mullser, by God' in great
delight. We were escorted into the kitchen where there was
a smell of bubbling bacon and a floury table under the
window where Mrs Noonan had been baking. The reunion
ended as I knew it would, with the vanishing of the two old
friends in the direction of Doyle's Corner, and Mrs Noonan
made tea for me which I didn't know how to refuse although
the steamy heat of the little place made me queasy. She said
Bernadette and Mollie and the four boys would be delighted
to meet me when they got back from Mass, and when I'd
somehow accounted for the tea I plucked up courage to ask
her if I could look over my father's old house. She seemed
surprised and indicated the small scullery off the room
where we were which had a door presumably leading to the
back. I thanked her and went through the tiny dark cave-
like scullery into the sunlight of about three square yards of
concrete. A door painted red presumably indicated the
lavatory – it was open to the air above and below. Apart
from two pots of geraniums, a dustbin, a galvanized bucket,
a water tap and a tiger tom cat who wasn't friendly, there
was nothing to see. The low walls indicated identical
concrete yards belonging to the houses next door. Compared
to this, our own undistinguished garden (which at least had
a tiny summer-house, an old tool shed, several shrubs and
a sycamore tree) was a paradise in which one could sit and
read on summer days. It would be difficult to sit out here.
I looked up at what was presumably the tiny square window
of a bedroom (my father's?) above the kitchen, but there
were no other windows. Was there in fact only one bedroom

which went through from front to back, and was it partitioned in the middle?

Back again in the house I noticed the small flight of steps
that looked really more like a ladder, leading up from the
kitchen into the upper storey, but there was suddenly a
sort of understanding between Mrs Noonan and myself that
what was beyond was none of my business. After my
interminable and rather embarrassing session with the
Noonan boys and girls, my father and his friend came back
merrily from their potations and my father issued a cordial
invitation to the whole family to visit us soon. He produced
his card, struck out the Gas Company's address in D'Olier
Street and substituted our own, before making his florid
farewells.

On the way home I sulked because I had been abandoned
but my father didn't even notice, so cheerful was he. Finally
curiosity overcame me and I asked him about the upstairs
regions.

He verified the absence of a bathroom and the fact that the
single bedroom was partitioned – where, I asked, did all
the children sleep? Half the partitioned room upstairs would
be occupied, he said, by the girls, since there were four of
them, and the other half by the parents. The two boys
probably had camp or chair beds which only made their
appearance at night in the kitchen. If there were more boys
than girls, then the girls would probably have the camp
beds, as had happened in his own family. He painted a jolly
picture of Saturday night scrubbing sessions in the scullery,
when his mother would fill the old hip bath with hot water
and allow each grown child ten minutes to conduct his
ablutions with Lifebuoy soap. The little ones – all in
America now – were bathed in front of the open fire in the
kitchen itself, and dried off in the warmth of the flames.

When I told my mother later of the visit she was amused
and (there is no other word) tender. 'He took me to see his
family for the first time the week before we were married
and I don't think I was ever in a happier house,' she said.

She was no snob my mother. She just had a highly developed sense of the fitness of things.

After the Carters went away to a new house in Monkstown and old Mrs Stapleton was found dead one morning in her bed, we were more islanded than ever. Boys and girls my own age left school and found work in Scott's jam factory or started to serve their time to their father's trade. I had no local friends who didn't regard me as a freak because I still went to school dressed in a black and white blazer and a crested beret. All my schoolfriends seemed to live miles away, in Clonskea or Rathgar or even in Dalkey. They travelled by train or car to school and occasionally I visited them for tea. My mother always insisted I invite them back in return and she usually turned out a spread that was far superior to anything I was given to eat in their houses. But their mothers could afford to be casual. They had big warm tiled kitchens down flights of steps from the hall, and in them were fridges and washing machines and larders and (in a few cases) even servants. They telephoned their order to the butcher or the grocer every day and their houses were so big that an extra child or two would hardly be noticed.

The girl I envied most had a carpeted room of her own overlooking a long lawn that sloped down to the sea. When you looked out from her old mahogany desk in the bay window, you could see the Hill of Howth across the bay, and near by on the lawn directly below were a sundial and a stone cupid rather foolishly holding a bird bath on his head. Fruit trees lined the red brick walls and there was a long curving rose bed. It was more orderly and more beautiful by far than my grandfather's garden could have been even in its heyday. Sometimes when a dense daytime fog blotted out everything beyond our tiny front garden, I daydreamed at my window, persuading myself that beyond the dripping privet hedge there was a long informal lawn with beech trees and soaring elms.

Sometimes I think my mother ceased to believe in the old

fairy-tale of one day owning her father's house, and these seemed to me the bad days. I didn't know that she was ill. I would come home from school to find her staring at nothing through the kitchen window, hands idle in her lap, some silly programme blaring from the BBC. In the beginning when she had at last acquired the precious piano, the time Mrs Stapleton's things were auctioned, she often played it when her scouring and polishing were finished. Not any more. Nobody except myself ever touched the piano now. The music lessons at school were only continued because I could never bring myself to tell her what a bore they were.

This day anyhow I had something to show her which I believed would cheer her up. I was feeling friendlier towards her than I had felt for weeks, being at that time going through the stage when I often hated my mother for my father's continuing delight in her company, for all the times he didn't even hear what I was saying because he thought she was waiting to speak. I felt at times he was unduly concerned about her altogether, making appointments with a specialist in Fitzwilliam Square when what he needed was a new pair of shoes for himself. Anyhow this day was just before the Christmas holidays and I had a thick shiny copy of the college annual which contained my first appearance in print – a painfully twee piece of sub-Wodehousian humour of which I was extraordinarily proud. 'Look on page seventeen,' I said casually to my mother. 'You may be surprised.' 'Later, Emily,' she said, 'I have so many things to do.' But she went on staring out through the window, merely moving one hand to prevent the bulky volume from slipping off her lap. Disgusted, I went up to my room, leaving her to Henry Hall's Dance Orchestra and 'The Way You Look Tonight'. She had never behaved so insufferably before.

Later on, of course, when my father and the boys came home there was great hilarity and my mother was pleased as Punch. She'd always known I'd do something to prove I was a cut above the rest even if my piano playing hadn't ever amounted to much. She bit her lip and giggled as though she were a girl again and she shot a triumphant look across the table at my father who was almost as delighted as she was. He went off to open one of the bottles of sherry he had hidden away for Christmas and we all had a glass to celebrate. I think it was the last time I ever heard my mother laugh. I know it was the last time I heard them making love in the bedroom next to mine. The war in Europe was three months old that Christmas, I remember.

Long before that war was over, my grandfather, my wild Uncle Dan, and my mother were all dead. But it had nothing to do with the war, with 'the Emergency' as Mr de Valera preferred to call it. 'The Gentleman', Dan, that grown-up spoiled baby, had been riding for a fall all his life, so people said. When he got it, however, it was self-inflicted, a fall indeed. He was found one April morning on the pavement where he had thrown himself from an attic room in Holles Street, just opposite the National Maternity Hospital. A young nurse on her way to work almost tripped over him and it was to that hospital he was ironically carried when there seemed to be some life left in him. But he died a few moments after his arrival and in the mortuary he was surrounded by the small bodies of stillborn babies. There was an inquest, and it was said by my Aunt Harriet that it would kill his father.

But my grandfather lived on even after Katy went back to Wexford to marry the farmer she had foolishly abandoned for Dan. After she had gone, the house in Drumcondra almost visibly crumbled. She had done nothing to maintain it except laugh and welcome anybody who knocked at the door, and when there was nobody to answer I used to go around by the back lane on my way home from school and call to my grandfather to let me in.

He still spent all his days messing with the cars in the old coach-house at the end of the wild garden. The tiny petrol ration had given new scope to his tinkering. He had con-

verted one of the cars to run on wood gas, generated in a
contraption like an old-fashioned iron stove clamped to the
back bumper, and he was using the remains of the other
car to try and develop an improved version. Whenever I
visited him I would end by dragging him up to the house
from his arduous and messy labours on the pretext of needing
a glass of milk after my hard day at school, but usually there
was no milk. I would make us a cup of tea on the 'glimmer'
and open a tin of condensed milk if I could find one. Sometimes, if I'd had a few pence, I would produce a couple of
sticky buns bought on my way past the Boston Bakery down
the road and my grandfather would make murmuring sounds
of approval as he used to long ago over hot buttered scones
by the fire at home, and he would suck his tea through the
fiery moustache. Always I would try to persuade him to
come home with me for a meal because my parents were
always so delighted to see him, however bad the war-time
shortages might be. About twice a week or so he would
come, roping my bike onto the old dicky seat behind and
rattling slowly and smokily around by Goose Green and
Philipsburgh Avenue, the way I had dreamily cycled that
morning with my eyes on the distant Sugarloaves. In the
summer he sometimes took my young brothers out to Dolly-
mount or Malahide, and sometimes my mother went too. I
was usually too busy with homework, but once or twice at
weekends we all went.

And then one day just before we broke up for the summer
holidays, there was no answer when I called again and again
from the back lane. The big lime tree that hung over the
wall was heavy with bees and there was no other sound
except a distant whirr of lawnmowers. I knew he was dead
and I knew where I would find him. Climbing up along the
branches of the lime tree with whatever foothold I could
contrive in the wall, I was quite certain I knew where I
would find him. And I was right. He lay face downwards
under the crank of the old Ford, which had probably kicked
harder than he had anticipated. I lifted one of the oily

chubby hands – the sort of hands you could never believe had supported his family by wielding a pen – and it fell like a stone from my own hand. He was already cold, and because I couldn't think what else to do I covered him with an old plaid rug from the car and went cycling home to tell my mother.

We went down to the public call box and phoned my father at work and he phoned the police, and then we went by taxi to Drumcondra. My mother never stopped crying. I wanted to tell her, 'Now you'll have what he always wanted you to have and you and I will make the house beautiful again,' but I didn't dare. I was past crying myself.

A few days after the funeral my mother was summoned to the solicitor's office and came back looking stunned. All that evening she lay on the old couch with her face to the wall, and that is more or less how I see her for the remainder of her life, which was only six months anyway. Her death certificate said carcinoma, but I think she would have died anyhow because our fine future had been indefinitely postponed.

There was my grandfather's will all right, dated ten years previously, leaving her the house and everything else he possessed, but an enormous mortgage had been taken out to cover Dan's debts. Even after the sale of the house, the slate would never be wiped clean, but with any luck we would not be responsible, the solicitor believed.

'It's not fair,' my mother said, her speckled blue eyes swimming in tears.

'It's not a fair world love,' said my father, 'but it's not the end of the world either. We'll have a lot of good times yet.'

But he knew what I knew, that the good times were all gone. For the foreseeable future, at any rate.